RENT GIRL

written by
Michelle Tea

illustrated by
Laurenn McCubbin

Contents

Ain't Nothin' But A Hooker Party   5

How I Hated Men   24

Boundaries   31

Body and Mind   59

I Like to Give Women Pleasure   74

Crabby   94

A Working Vacation in Tucson   114

Dusted   130

Tattoo You   145

Pluto Drive - San Francisco   158

Dedications

Michelle
For Rocco Kayiatos

Laurenn
For Sherrill Jean and Jenna Rochelle

Rent Girl

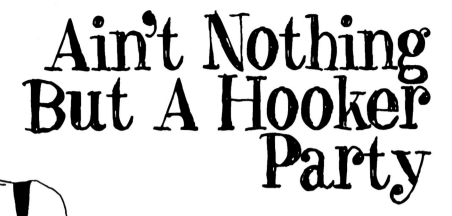

Ain't Nothing But A Hooker Party

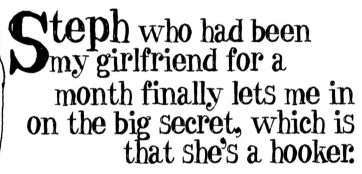

Steph who had been my girlfriend for a month finally lets me in on the big secret, which is that she's a hooker.

This brings me into the exclusive clique of people who know: Steph, Steph's best friend Dinah—also a hooker—and our friend Amy, who is not. Yet. And so the four of us get to go to the totally invite-only hooker party in the big hotel down by the water.

Before her revelation, Steph was full of lies. So many nights she could not see me. She had to baby sit all the time or she had plans with old friends I didn't know and would be bored by or else she had to cater a wedding, standing behind a hot plate of Swedish meatballs in a smock and a smile. She told me she worked a bunch of odd jobs but really she only worked one, the oddest—an escort, which equals prostitute. It was with amazement that I learned that my girlfriend, with whom I kissed, snuggled, and fought, upon whom I chewed and slurped, was a hooker. It made me like her even more, it sealed everything. If there were any lingering doubts that I was on the right path with this lesbian thing, Steph's revelation banished them. A lesbian call-girl. My girlfriend.

I was twenty-one years old

but inside I felt thirty, thirty-one. I hated revealing my age to anyone because it gave them the wrong idea about me. It gave them the idea that I was young when inside I felt ageless, that I didn't know much when really I knew more then they did. I thought that I felt thirty-one, thirty-two years old, but I was wrong. Now that I am thirty-two I can feel how it feels, and it does not feel twenty-one. So I was the sort of twenty-one year old who believes that deep in their soul they are thirty, thirty-five, which really is such a twenty-one year old way to think. And here is my lesbian prostitute girlfriend. She has a real female body, womanly because she's twenty-seven already, and I have a child's body, straight flat all the way down with a couple of puckers for tits, like someone meanly pinched the skin there, gave it a yank and it stayed that way.

When Steph confessed she thought she was copping to being only one thing, an escort, but she was of course also revealing herself to be a liar, something neither of us understood at the time. I understood that this world was a weasly world, it was cruel and forced compromise on everyone, and often the first thing to go was the truth. Like, you'd like to be free and open with the facts but you simply can't, because you'll get grounded or fired, or your kids will be taken away or your girlfriend will break up with you.

I understood lying to be a survival skill, but after listening to Steph tell the woman that she did occasionally nanny for that she couldn't come in because her brother had been struck by a car and killed—it lodged a suspicion, a bit of doom, in my heart. A magnetized sliver of grimness that drew to it every lie Steph would tell, getting chunkier and heavier as time went on. My mouth hung open as Steph spoke into the telephone receiver, details about blood and bone, and her voice was numb with trauma. A little catch of dryness at the back of her throat, like the muscle that was holding back the torrent was spasming, weakening, and the woman had better let her off the phone fast, which she did.

What do you say when your nanny calls in sick with a car crash death?

You say oh my god and oh no and you say okay. Steph hung up the phone and smiled triumphant and laughed and said, Was that terrible? and I didn't know whether she meant what she had done or her delivery, her acting ability. Was that terrible? It was convincing. Steph really did have a brother and personally I was too superstitious to tell such a lie, a death-lie about a living, breathing relative you love, but I was twenty-one and I admired Steph for doing it, for tempting fate, the universe, a punishing god—was there no one she would not fuck with? No, there was no one with whom Steph would not fuck with, and I thought that perhaps with such a person beside me I could be safe inside this weasly world of cruelty and compromise.

Steph says Get dressed, we're going to the escort party.

Steph always called her business escorting, and referred to herself and the others as escorts. Her roommate Dinah was an escort and thus going to the escort party, and Amy was coming along too though like me she was not an escort—not yet an escort. It is nearly impossible to hang out with hookers and not want to give it a try yourself, especially if the hookers you're hanging out with seem totally unscarred and glamorous and financially secure.

What to wear to the hooker party?

I wore this dress I'd thrifted, I was practically living in it then, it was my favorite dress. A simple black dress with big red roses all over it. It looked homemade. Some little black shoes. Steph wore one of the silk, floor-sweeping dresses she took calls in. Like her body beneath, the dresses were very womanly. Normally when Steph went out, to gallery openings or discos, she wore things like cutoff jeans and a bra. It was the early nineties. This being a work function she donned the fancy flowing floral formal, and heels.

Dinah wore something similarly—and, I thought, strangely, considering their line of work—conservative. They looked like young society marrieds.

Amy looked like a sloppy, raggedy dyke, and the two of us pledged to stick close to each other—a girl in obviously used clothing and a girl who was not at first glance a girl, crashing the invite-only hooker party on a Friday night.

The hotel was a big chain, like a Sheraton or a Marriot, and it was in Boston, down on one of the wharfs.

The night sky was enormous and filled with harbor smells, salty and maybe fresh, maybe sour. The water banged up against the squat wooden piers, there were ocean noises, a wet lapping, things that clanked rhythmically with the slap of the tide. The four of us clattered up the wide brick courtyard that led to the giant hotel. Or rather Steph and Dinah and I clattered and Amy stomped. Please do not misunderstand me, Amy was not butch, not at all, but nor was she femme.

Amy was just a dyke. So cute.

Wiggly teeth, a gap in the front that made it look like her mouth was winking at you when she smiled. She wore glasses, and her hair was half static, half cowlicks. She was gangly, and the thick and spongy soles of her boots made her even taller. We entered the hotel and sunk into the carpet, swished toward the in-hotel nightclub which I think was called Chances. Maybe Wishes. Faces. It had some sort of gaybar-sounding name but it was not gay. Not that night anyway. Steph and Dinah showed their invites to a beefy, neckless man at the door. He looked plainly at them for a second, then turned his gaze pointlessly away, admitting them without a word or a glance. His face was deliberately unreadable, perhaps a bit resigned, like he had an opinion about this here party tonight oh yeah he did, but it sure wasn't worth losing his job over. I was surprised. I'd sized him up quickly and had been steeling myself for some lewd harassment, trying to quickly calculate a scathing retort to the leering I expected. But no. I wasn't sure what was worse, being quietly judged, or sexualized and hit on. Duh, Steph said, Are you stupid? Quietly judged. Dinah nodded. Quietly judged.

The inside of Chances- Wishes- Faces was a fantastic blur, light bouncing off mirror into infinity.

Would I have a seizure? I would have a drink. The bar was wide open. As if the promise of being in a room chock-full of actual prostitutes —prostitutes, a being that had occupied a magical mental territory ever since I was old enough to watch cable television in the 80s—as if this was not enough, there was also free booze. Free booze and hookers. The ultimate drabness of my outfit was revealed within the nightclub's flashing splendor. I melted into a comfortable obscurity. I was hardly there, I might as well have been a man. It was an interesting experience, entirely new. I was twenty-one years old and wore short skirts with regularity, I was always in someone's vision. Not at this party. I was there to get drunk and gawk at prostitutes, just like the men. I clutched a chunky glass filled with vodka and ice. Look at her look at her look at her, Amy kept jabbing me. We were at the edge of the dance floor, leaning on the brass railing that encircled it. The dance floor itself was lit from within with colored lights that spun and rolled. Girls danced atop it.

I was surprised to see that the women looked like hookers.

I mean, if someone nudged you and said, that girl's a hooker, you would be like, duh. Since Steph's disclosure I had been busy dismantling my stereotypes about prostitutes, re imagining the mythical whore as someone who looked and dressed, more or less, like my girlfriend. Kind of regular, well-bred, bland. Not punk or trampy. The girls boogying down on the elaborate dance floor had bodies that shook inside tight spandex dresses, had ass cheeks that threatened to roll out from under miniature denim skirts, had legs stuck in a permanent flex from the steep slope of their stilettos. Whoa, I breathed. Amy could not hear me over the music, the early nineties dance hits, Janet Jackson, Bobby Brown—who, by the way, was a supposed client of this particular agency and maybe, the rumor flew, would be stopping by. He did not.

Amy's eyes were glued to the ladies,

her lips gently parted around her wonky teeth. Was she hot for them, I wondered? Amy had a girlfriend with whom she always fought about lingerie. She wanted her girlfriend to wear some, her girlfriend would not. Maybe Amy was butch. Look at her, she turned my shoulder to a woman with chemical yellow hair bobbing in sprayed curls around her neck. Tons of eye makeup and stone washed jeans. I hadn't seen girls like this since high school, I'd forgotten they existed. It had been three years since graduation, and now I knew only punks or lesbians or punk lesbians. I didn't know anyone who wore stone washed jeans. Stone washed jeans with little stone washed bows stuck at the tip of the slit in the ankle. Whoa. The woman wearing them moved her feet and her tall shoes became lost in the shine of the lit-up floor, a blur.

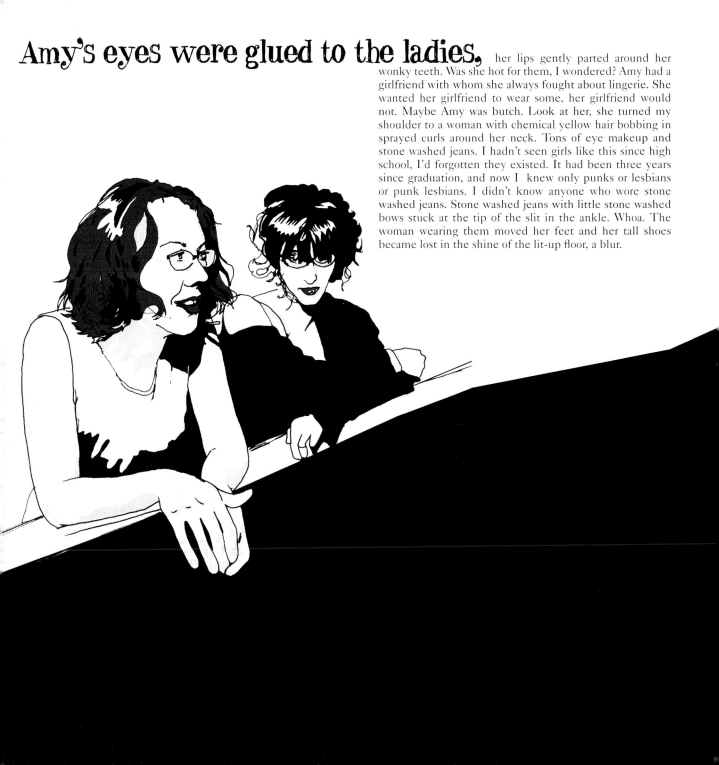

I was sort of drunk, could be drunker.

I looked at Amy, Her pint glass was empty. Come On, I tugged her. We'd gotten to the party later then planned because Steph had to smoke pot before we left and the time-consuming stoner ritual of separating the seeds, packing the pipe. The bar was only open for another half-hour or so. Beer Is Money, I said sternly to my friend, and we rimmed the edge of the dance floor, the curving carpeted path to the bar.

We passed many men who looked like Middle Eastern football players.

They were mustached and broad, in dark suits. They looked at Amy and me briefly, and looked away. At the bar we waited desperately as the bartender served everyone but us. Did we look like non-tipping freeloaders or what? Order a double, suggested a sage Amy. Eventually the bartender acknowledged us, eventually I was gazing into my double shot greedily. Soon I would be very drunk. Steph and Dinah ran up behind us, Dinah holding a skinny cocktail, Steph wearing her bleary, stoned eyes.

Oh my god! she gushed. This place is filled with frrrrreaks.

Steph had this great and terrible way of saying the word 'freak.' She rolled the Rs out forever and made it sound like both the funnest thing to call someone and truly the worst thing a person could be called, a frrrreak. As someone who had been called such a thing for many years in high school, who still qualified as a freak in most judging and resentful New England enclaves, I was shocked to hear it as my girlfriend's favorite insult. I myself preferred jeers that ridiculed a person's lack of intelligence and the base cruelty that tends to accompany such ignorance. Words like stupid, idiot, stupid idiot, jerk, jock, and fascist. Fascist was my favorite because saying it makes the spit want to fly from your mouth, but it is such a heavy insult, you have to use it sparingly or else people won't take you seriously. Frrrrreaks, Steph trilled again, delighted.

You've got to meet Lynn, the boss. The madame. The Madame! I gasped. It's her birthday, Dinah reminded. The reason everyone was dancing their acid-washed hot pants off here on the lit-up dance floor of Chances-Wishes-Faces at the Long Wharf Marriott-Sheraton-Hilton. Wherever the fuck we were.

I was ready to meet the madame, the queen, queen of the hookers.

Her hair flipped about her head in a series of precision-cut wings, the feathers keeping their daring arrangement with what I could only imagine was a lot of Super Extra Hold Aqua Net. Teased high, a big hairdo from the late 80s, bleached a buttery blonde. Her pouchy face dusted with powders, with rouge, her dress a shimmering tide of sequins and beads. She was talking to a large and swarthy man , and as we approached she turned from him and spread her arms in welcome at the sight of Steph and Dinah. Steph was pulling a small wrapped box from her purse, Happy birthday! she and Dinah cheered in unison. My girls! rasped the madame. She had the gravelly old voice of career smoker, but she was young. That's what was startling—Lynn the madame, queen of the hookers, looked not much older then me. She could not be thirty years old, she looked younger even then Steph, who at the age of twenty-seven qualified as an Older Woman, at least in my private world. I gaped in awe at the small-framed young female, the unlikely head of this empire of cash and women, the holder of the power. I could no longer think of her as 'madame', which conjured images of Dolly Parton, a woman of her shape and age and aesthetic. Lynn looked indistinguishable from the girls dancing back on the swirly disco dance floor.

She reeled Steph and Dinah in for a clutch and turned back to the man. These girls got real class, she told him, giving them a playful shake. My classiest, these two. Steph and Dinah looked at each other, biting back giggles. Talk about being a big fish in a little pond. It wasn't hard to look classy at Chances. It wasn't hard to look classy, feel snobby. Oh, you guys! Lynn shook the small gift and slipped it into her own beaded purse. Don't spend your hard-earned money on me! Some people do not open their birthday presents right away. I don't understand those sorts of people. They like to open them later, home alone. It's so weird. It was just a necklace, Steph said. A big L on a chain.

Later, when Steph got me a job at Lynn's agency, Lynn laughed and said, That little one? With nothing up top and all the earrings? You girls are crazy! Sure, we'll give her a try.

After the party we went down to Sully's to continue drinking. A little Irish bar in the dark and cobbled streets that wound cramped and old-worldly behind the big department stores downtown. Irish cops drank there, and underage punk kids, bike messengers, and, occasionally, Aimee Mann and Peter Wolfe. We squeezed into a tight booth in the back room with Dinah's current boyfriend, a motorcycle guy named Chris. Chris was okay. He was quiet.

He was such a man, not a boy or a guy.

I thought it was strange. What does Dinah do with him, I wondered. I am such a lesbian. I wobbled up to the hole in the wall where the back room ordered its drinks. A red, Irish guy approached impatiently. A greyhound and a bag of chips. It was something like two dollars. Unbelievably cheap to drink at Sully's, and the guy hadn't carded. This was important information. I was twenty-one but certain friends of mine weren't yet. Sully's Don't Card. That's what you'd say. I brought my cocktail and salty snack back to the booth, inserted my bony legs into the leg-puzzle jabbing beneath the narrow table. The thing about the cocktails at Sully's is they were cheap but gone in a flash, and it wasn't just because they served a population prone to alcoholism. The glasses were so tiny, glorified shot glasses crammed with ice. But they made their drinks wicked strong. I couldn't tell whether it was a good deal or not, drinking at Sully's but who cared. The night had been a deal already, with all the free alcohol at the hooker party. I Drank Soooo Much Alcohol At That Crazy party! I hooted, reaching for my cigarettes. A sharp-toed shoe gouged my shin, then dropped its heel onto my toe for emphasis. What party, Chris asked, confused. Oh Michelle had to go to some weird party out in Chelsea earlier, Steph provided a quick lie. My body tingled with a rising flush that traveled the length of my drunken body. Oh shit. That was so close. They'd just let me in on their hooker secret and I almost ruined Dinah's life, right there in front of her boyfriend. He couldn't know that Dinah was a hooker. He was a guy, he'd never understand.

How was it? he asked politely. Oh, It Was Fun, I shrugged lightly, embarrassed. Lots of free alcohol? Steph asked. Are you drunk? Her blue eyes flashed like the dance floor at Chances. Yeah, I'm Drunk, I laughed, and shakily pulled a cigarette from my pack. You, Steph said teasingly, like an old movie star or a fag.

You're always drunk aren't you?

I wanted to snap back that Steph was always stoned but it was useless, we'd had the fight before and Steph seemed to think that because pot was a plant that grew naturally from the ground and that people stoned on it didn't tend to kill people in car accidents that it was fine to start smoking it with your morning coffee and continue as needed throughout the rest of the day. Steph grinned a sly, stoned grin at me. She was actually flirting with me, I realized with horror. When Steph flirted she got very girly, she flirted with me like a clawed kitten and I did not know what to do with it. I could only squirm and drink more. Nothing made me feel less sexy and more confused. It made no sense—if I was a lesbian—which has already been determined from my absolute bewilderment in the face of Chris and other men—why didn't I like my girlfriend flirting with me? I lit my cigarette, let it do my breathing for me. Frrrreak, Steph purred softly. Treacherous, I thought. A treacherous table. I drained my greyhound. Next round's on me, Steph declared, and stood.

How I Hated Men

Not every woman in the sex industry was sexually abused. As for me, I was, and then I wasn't.

My therapist informed me that what happened in my house is to be filed under Sexual Inappropriateness. The sort of stuff that could get your family put under the hawkish watch of Social Services, but not enough to get you removed from your parents. Not enough to get anyone flung in jail. So it was a big deal, and then it wasn't a big deal. I don't wake up in the middle of the night with cold sweat and a phantom indentation haunting my mattress. It's more like I trusted someone completely who turned out to have a secret and deeply creepy preoccupation with that female thing I have, my body. There was a huge betrayal, enormous like a meteor crater that *wham!* made my family extinct.

I am trying to give you a landscape, a crumpled map.

I am trying to extract, thread by thread, the causes and preoccupations that provided me with the willingness to pursue this occupation. I wanted to try things, everything, especially things that are illegal and have a faint whiff of glamour. I remember being on a school trip to Boston in the early 80s and every kid on the Catholic schoolbus was nose-flat against the windows looking for 'hookers.' Never mind that there was a brisk skin trade in our own city, Chelsea. My uncle's girlfriend, who was a series of superlatives as in the prettiest face the biggest hair and the worst teeth I've ever seen, she worked the streets down in Chelsea Square. But all the sad and shabby women like her, mostly on drugs, walking a crooked walk through the badder part of our bad town, they didn't resonate as 'hooker.'

What were we looking for? Think Donna Summer, toot-toot, yeah, beep-beep.

There's A Hooker! one of the boys jabbed the smudgy pane. Outside was a woman waiting to cross the street. She had big, stormy hair and a shiny, tiny outfit. Her heels were tall. Maybe she was a hooker or maybe it was just 1982. But I nodded at the window, took in the brief length of her skirt, the point of her shoes, all that bright makeup and this great look on her face, sort of dreamy, spacing out while waiting for the light to change, confident in her extreme outfit, deeply engaged with herself. Walking the streets alone in stilettos, a hooker. I sighed.

Inappropriate step dad or no, I could have wound up hooking, but it helped to have been intensely fucked over by the man I considered my father. Men are all evil, I thought, except for the ones too pathetic to be anything as grand as that. They are gross, base and absolutely never to be trusted, not ever, even when they act okay to your face. You just don't know what they're up to once you turn your ass on them. It also helped that I was queer. I didn't really have any reason to try to not hate men, and it didn't seem like the men of the world, or at least of New England, were interested in helping me not hate them—I mean, the streets were teeming with assholes. So there, men are losers.

I felt sort of resigned and hopeless after the thing with my stepfather came out.

The only justice I managed to mete out was destroying his porn collection.

It wasn't a lot—a few Hustlers, a couple Playboys, all stashed in his top dresser drawer. I ripped them up and stuck Queer Nation stickers on the centerfolds. Steph was with me. We couldn't believe how awful some of it was. Racist cartoons, or cartoons with roaches crawling into a women's snatch. A fuck pictorial featuring a lady Indian and a conquering Englishman in a powdery white wig. Steph harvested a lot of the pages for a zine she planned on making about how bad porn is. She was going to call it Porn Zine. She never made it. Steph had a lot of good ideas, but she smoked too much pot.

I took up a vegan diet because I was suddenly incredibly, painfully sensitive to how cruel it is to the animals. I understood that I am the animals. Milk tasted sour in my mouth, tasted animal, and the butter in cookies coated my tongue, made me gag. I was having this awful breakdown that feels almost mystical, I could see my own struggle in every other struggle. There was no difference between my mother siding with my stepfather and a factory worker searing the beak off a chicken. My vegan diet was very kind, but it kept me in a state of chronic low-blood sugar. Which never helps.

I had to move out of my parent's house because I couldn't be around my stepfather. I was twenty-one so I guess it was time but really, I wasn't ready. My family wobbles between poor and working-class. No one had gone to college. I tried, but it was too much, I didn't get it. My sister would be the first and only to graduate. She stayed in the house and deals with the injustice of our stepfather by making him bring her home jars of pickles. I moved in with Steph. We'd only been going out for a month and that's exactly how long she'd been gay for. I was thrilled to meet someone who had been gay for less time then I had. I was sick of being the newest lesbian, and now I was relieved of this role by Steph.

We had met outside an abortion clinic, I liked her for how mean she was to the Christians.

I didn't think she was that mean to everyone, but I would find out. I moved into her house cause I had nowhere to go. I was working as a receptionist at a hair salon. It's not a nice one, it's a supercutsy place that doesn't pull in much money. I got a second job, at the Middle Eastern cafe across the street from my first job. I work and work and at night I smell like either Spritz Forte or olive oil and garlic. My boss at the hair salon let me have free haircuts and color cellophanes, but my boss at the cafe wouldn't let me snack from the vats of hummus and olives and falafel.

There was a very short span of time between Steph explaining that she worked as a prostitute and me joining her. I quit the hair salon and I quit the cafe. Once I was hooking I could afford to eat there, could buy myself a haircut. I had so much money, and I hated the men so much. It was the only way it could be. To have compassion for them would kill me. I could feel a tender sadness, like the one I carried for the cows and the chickens, hovering somewhere near my heart, but to allow its existence would require me to forgive my stepfather, would permit a flood of compassion for the world and the world, far as I could see, was cruel. Every day I was witness to the worst of men. Their carelessness and grand entitlement. The way they can so profoundly disconnect from what it is they're having sex with, the way they think they own the world, watch them purchase a female. I was witness to their deep delusions. Spoiled babies all of them, and so many of them called prostitutes. I thought, maybe all men called prostitutes. It was a terrible thought, but really, what did I care. There was a system in place that was older and stronger then I could begin to imagine. Who was I? I was just a girl. What was I going to do about it. If I had any power I would make it so that nobody was ever bought or sold or rented and that chickens kept their beaks and cows could lie and nurse their baby cows with all that milk, but I didn't have any power. I would ride the system until it knocked me off. I would get as much money as I could and feed my hate like a glutton. I had found the perfect job for both.

In-Call, Out-Call, Boston, Massachusetts

Boundaries

Marina's hair was red and curly and she dyed her pubes to match, though I don't know who she thought she was fooling. Marina was synthetic.

Even her name might be fake, the name she adopted to whore with.

It has been a long time and I don't know if Marina is living or dead. Her thick makeup gave her the look of an airbrushed mural on the side of a van, or a Nagel painting. Darkened eyes, canyons of red up the side of her cheeks, lips drippy with thick red gloss. Marina's nails were polished talons, and she really did dress like a whore. She looked the part and it worked for her. A lot of men wanted the women rented to have a wholesome air about them, the fresh-faced, I'm-Putting-Myself-Through-College schtick. I guess it made it seem more like a healthy, all-American male tradition, maybe even a kindhearted act of charity, a sort of student loan. But Marina, she looked like a street hooker from a cheesy 80s cop drama, and it worked for her. We worked together at the in-call on Comm Ave., and she got tons of call, lots of them regulars. One guy out on Cape Cod really loved her. He would have her drive all the way up Massachusetts' curling arm with a packet of cocaine in her purse. She would sit in a negligee and tell him stories.

Cocaine calls really reminded you why you were a whore. They were the best. There was one, David Smith, all the whores were tracking his steady, drug-propelled demise. By the time Lynn sent me on an out-call to his apartment there was hardly anything left in it, just a clean, round table, a microwave, his bed and his television. I sat on the bed in front of the flickering television and David clutched the remote—flick, flick, flick, never resting on a program for more than a few seconds. This went on for seven hours. It was my longest call ever, and the easiest. David was slumped on the bed looking really unhappy; occasionally he let the screen rest on a particular show—CSPAN coverage of a senate race in Virginia, a western, boring stuff. He would pass through something good—Heathers was on, and Donohue, lots of nature programs, and I would pipe up Hey That's A Good One, but he'd already zipped through it.

Nothing good's on, nothing good's ever on, David chanted, transfixed by the box.

David was your average white businessguy, middle-aged, still in his button-down work shirt but without the tie. I may have run into him a dozen times before or since and I would not remember, the guy was that average.

This is how the call went: under the bed was a round ceramic dinner plate dotted with little mounds of coke. I took David Smith's credit card and I chopped and chopped the stuff into a fine powder. I sculpted them into good fat lines. I presented the plate to David Smith, who pulled himself up on his elbows, pulled out a rolled up bill and sucked it up his nose.

Take off your clothes, he said, and the ritual began.

Winter in Boston, way out in Newton I think he lived and I had this tremendously long black velvet coat, looped all over with fancy black embroidery.

It was a beautiful coat, a queen's coat. Under it was some kind of dress probably belonging to my Steph who, being wealthy from birth, owned lots of tasteful, feminine outfits, flowing rayon things with floral prints and gold buttons. These dresses were all too big for me, but since they never stayed on long it didn't really matter. Black panties, black garter belt, black stockings, a tiny black bra.

I was naked on
David Smith's
bed.

He dove for my pussy, his fingers blunt and frenzied with cocaine. I kept my thighs clenched tight to protect my clit from his fumblings, arched my back and pretended to come. I hollered a little, bucked his hands straight off me with my dramatic orgasm and David Smith went back to his television and did not touch me again. Seven hours I was there. I would lie out his freshly pulverized drugs, and smoke his cigarettes, Marlboros.

I chain-smoked them. I did not do his other drugs.

I walked into his empty kitchen and went through his cabinets.

They were empty too. What did the guy eat? I n
his freezer were a couple of TV dinners
for kids, and I found a full jar of pickles
in the refrigerator. I took it back into the
bedroom where David was attacking the
remote control.

Can I Eat These?
I asked. Uh, he grunted.

David Smith was paranoid.

Sssshhhh . . . he'd start, muting the television. Ssssh, ssshhh, ssshhh, did you hear that? Did you hear that? We sat together in the quiet. Nnnoooo . . . I'd venture hesitantly. I Don't Hear Anything. Sssshhhh, sssshhhh, ssshhhh. It's my ex-wife. It's my ex-wife. The plate of coke went back under the bed. Check the doors, check the house.

I padded naked
through the empty apartment,
double checking the locks and peeking in the closets.

His paranoia was contagious in the creepy, vacant apartment. I rushed back to the TV. No One's Here, David. You checked the locks? Yes, I Checked The Locks, It's OK. I cut him some more coke and ate his pickles, smoked. The luxury of eating an entire jar of pickles. I polished it off and sipped from the juice. David's paranoia returned. Sssshhhh sssshhh sssshhh. It's the cops, the cops are here. Want Me To Check The House, David? My voice was soothing. I made my rounds through the apartment.

Every hour on the hour I had to collect the next hour's cash up front. David, Do You Want Me To Stay Another Hour? I'd ask him this three or four times before he'd answer. Yeah. I Need The Money Right Now If You Want Me To Stay. That soothing voice again, the one for crazy people, babies and tricks. Now It's Time To Pay Me. Sssssshhh, sssshhh, ssshhh, he'd start that shit again. David, I Need The Money. Sssshh, sssshhhh ssshhhh. No sssshhhhhh David, If You Don't Pay Me Right Now I'm Leaving. He was a zombie, his eyes flashing with the television's reflection. He was spending a lot of money to have a really bad time. Up I went, picking my bits of clothing off the floor, pulling on the stockings, hitching them up to the garter, snapping on the bra, the dress, the heavy coat, maybe even a scarf, my purse flung dramatically over my shoulder—Bye Bye David, I'm Leaving Now, Goodbye! Here, here, he reached into his pocket, his front pants pocket, and pulled out a tremendous roll of bills. Now that I was a whore I was able to really recognize what a lot of money looked like, and that was a lot of money. I nearly moaned. He peeled a couple off and tossed them at me, shoved the riches back in his pocket. Oh, the thoughts that went through my head. Murder, duh, I could kill him, sure I could. A knife from the kitchen, or a frying pan if he had such appliances. Knock him out, grab the roll. The mind of a whore is a mind of hate and greed. At least mine was.

I took my clothes back off and sat down on the bed, prepared myself for another hour of manic channel-changing and paranoid outbursts.

I sat and smoked and fantasized about David Smith dying.

When the hour was up we went through it again. I'd ask for the cash, he'd get paranoid, I'd get dressed and dramatically say good-bye, and he'd reach his hand into the golden pocket. I did this seven times. I made a bunch of money. I could have stayed the whole next day. I didn't want to believe it when he finally let me go. He had an ultimate paranoia moment—the TV got shut off, the lights went out and we lay motionless on the dark bed, side by side, the digital clock flicking its glowing numbers. Top of the hour, four, maybe five AM. David I Have To Go, I whispered. He grunted. David, You Have To Pay Me Blah Blah Blah, I launched into the routine but David was out. Maybe asleep. But he was on all that coke, lines and lines of the stuff. Maybe he was dead. That seemed more likely. Was he breathing? He was quiet. Now was the time to steal his money, but I didn't. I just got out of that empty, creepy apartment. I had seven hundred dollars, I was rich.

But wasn't this about Marina?

She would do those coke calls out on Cape Cod, with a guy who looked like the White Rabbit, kind of startled pink with white hair. Marina would bring a friend and everyone would do coke and talk dirty. The girls would, I don't know, eat whipped cream off each other's pussy, and the guy would jerk off. He wouldn't touch them. He wanted to hear incest stories. Eeeeh, I said. I stayed away from those calls. It was so hard to maintain boundaries in this job, incest and little-girl fantasies were the one taboo I held fast to, one situation I could clearly identify and say no to.

RED HOT ACTION
incall - 555-1212

TEEN DREAM
incall - 555-1212

And then Lynn headlined my ad in the back pages of The Boston Phoenix 'Teen Dream.'

I wanted to kill her. Lynn who was actually younger than me, nineteen years old and running the in-call, even taking calls in the rooms when she wasn't over at Boston University working on her MBA. Her Teen Dream ad had every pedophile in the city calling me, and I got them often enough with my tiny measurements. I couldn't believe she'd decided to capitalize on my womanless physique without asking first. I pitched a giant fit, and my tiny newsprint square was given the new heading College Co-Ed. I didn't go to college and never would, but it was, of course, an industry of illusion. Giving my ad the headline Confused Lesbian Slacker With No Saleable Job Skills wouldn't have worked.

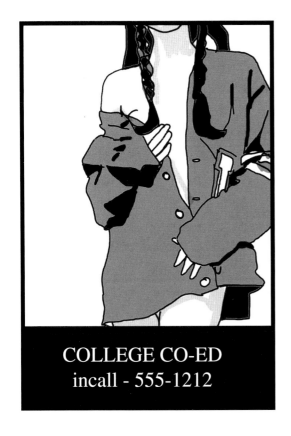

COLLEGE CO-ED
incall - 555-1212

**CONFUSED LESBIAN
SLACKER WITH NO
SALEABLE JOB SKILLS**
incall - 555-1212

Marina had been abused by her dad when she was a girl, and she'd do coke and tell this guy about it as he jerked off.

Marina! I gasped. I was astonished. She didn't really care. It gave me flutters of anxiety, her blasé admission, the idea of the creepy man getting off on the rehashing of a child's abuse. Maybe the anti-sex industry feminists were right, maybe this was evil work, work that tore the fragile scabbing of every wound a girl ever got, again and again, till pain felt regular, felt like nothing. Maybe we were encouraging the worst of men, helping blur their already schizophrenic line between fantasy and reality, what they're allowed to have and what they're not. I knew that some girls thought we were actually preventing rape and incest by giving the men a consensual space to act out their fantasies, and it grossed me out beyond belief to think I was fucking would-be sex criminals, but I believed them. What I didn't believe that any of us, with our cheesy one-hour sex routines, would be enough to keep these men from hurting a female if that's what they wanted to do. And what I secretly wondered was, were we empowering them sexually to go and do just that. Go and do just anything they wanted.

So I tried to have standards, to construct boundaries and limitations that I hoped would keep me sane and keep my karma free from the possible havoc a man could wreak after fucking me. No little-girl calls, no incest, and I would not lick a guy's butt. Amy did, and I was horrified. Actually I felt responsible. For everything. All the time. In case you haven't noticed. It's a great coping mechanism for powerless people, cultivating a grand delusion of overwhelming power. And I had brought Amy into this business and Steph had ushered me. I hooked Amy up with Lynn, taught her how to dress like a straight girl, packed her clutch purse full of condoms and lube. I had failed to mention ass-licking. Amy, Don't Do That! I exclaimed. You Don't Have To Do That! Really? She thought she had to do whatever they wanted her to. After all, they were paying her. The butt guy was an out-call, I saw him right after Amy did,

our giggling paths crossing in the lushly carpeted hallway of some blue-blooded Bostonian hotel.

His room service tray was a gleaming mess in the middle of the room: desiccated chicken bones, a thin film of mashed potato ringing the edge of the china. An uneaten roll, a pat of butter, wine. My stomach growled. Hotel calls always tempted me to indulge in some Little Princess sort of fantasy, as if some of the luxury—room service, hot tub, cocktails from the mini-bar—would be shared with me, but they never were. Once a guy let me have the miniature soaps and shampoos from the bathroom, but that was it. But this guy, ass-guy, he just sprawled out on his soft belly, offering me his whitest butt cheeks, which I kneaded like dough, gazing at that one perfect roll on the tray, the dusting of flour on its crust. Lick my asshole. Excuse Me? My insides jumped as if I'd been insulted. I'm Sorry, I Don't Do That. The last girl did it, she did a great job. I thought of Amy, her large, square teeth, the kiddish gap in the center. Well, I'm Sorry, I Don't Do That. For Christ's sake, you're not going to catch anything. It's not a big deal. Now I was definitely not licking the asshole's asshole. Sorry, I said curtly.

How about fifty dollars, I'll give you fifty dollars if you lick my asshole.

I thought about it.

Fifty dollars was almost half of what I'd get for fucking him. But oh god surely it would be so much worse then fucking him. I thought, for three hundred dollars I would do it with a dental dam. I told him. Three hundred dollars and a what? I gave him a blowjob. As I felt the condom fatten with liquid I thought, is there even a difference? It seemed stupid to say some acts were okay and others off-limits when they all were so disgusting.

When Lynn booked me a call with Marina's coked-out regular, down from Cape Cod for a business meeting in Boston, I told her straight up that I wasn't going to tell him stories. I tried not to talk to these men at all, tried to exert as little energy as possible. I could never be a stripper. You use so much of yourself, your brain, your muscles. It was exhausting for me just to lie there beneath them, emitting an occasional moan. As it happened, Marina's regular didn't want me to tell him stories, he wanted to tell me stories. He was behind me on the bed, on his side, fucking me like that, from behind. He was telling me all about getting fucked by his big sister. I just let him jabber, let him ramble, keeping quiet. I didn't want to talk about this shit with this man, this old, white-haired man. His older sister, if he even had one, was old now, too; an elderly woman, perhaps dead, perhaps demented in a nursing home. They're just harmless fantasies, one of the girls I worked with had said, and probably she was right. But still it chafed me, these guys and their fantasies that often resembled nightmares. Oh, you're just a man-hating lesbian! she had swatted at my arm. Truly, yes, I was. And I thought, these men don't deserve the pleasure of a fantasy life, of an imagination, of a sexual experience. But even Amy, who had now adopted my no-butt-licking standard, thought I was uptight about the fantasies.

I nodded miserably. I did too, and sweet Amy had them, and every asshole who walked through the doors at the Comm Ave. cathouse had them, and every man who opened his front door to me, brushing me quickly into his house. We were all just fucked in the head. The White Rabbit guy was taking forever coming, and I knew it was because I was so silent, not there. If I wanted to thing to end I would have to participate. What Else Did your Big Sister Do To You? As far as fantasies went, it was pretty tame. If it was a fantasy. And the fucking was beginning to feel good, which then made me feel sick, a roar of shame and rage as full as any orgasm.

The trick left and Marina was there, in the brothel, on the black couch that looked like leather but was actually this thin, shiny cotton. Why Didn't You See Him? I asked. I was booked, she chirped. He's a sweetie, huh?

Marina had a boyfriend, and the boyfriend was a cop.

Incredibly, he thought she only answered our telephones. They would go on double dates with our boss Lynn and her boyfriend Mark, the four of them hanging out at some awful, townie Boston sports bar, drinking beer and eating buffalo wings.

Across the street from the building which contained
our illicit apartment was an alley which led to a lot,
and the lot was filled with pigeons. Often they were
dead or really fucked up, and Marina adopted one
of the sicker, mutant ones. She gave it some long
Italian name. It lived in a little cage on top of
the TV, which meant you couldn't watch TV
because you didn't want to look at the bird.
It must've gotten hit by a car, it was just
mangled. Head twisted back, feathers
broken and it could barely walk. I
don't understand how it just didn't
die. Marina would take it out of
the cage and cuddle it into her
cleavage, coo at it. She would
feed it with an eyedropper. Once
she left it out on the table, and it
was trying to walk but it could only
move backwards and so it fell off the
table, hitting the floor with a thud
and a squawk. I couldn't look. I heard
it struggling to get up, a shuffling,
scratching sound. Marina! I screamed,
Marina, The Bird Fell! She was in the
bathroom, getting ready for a call. She
ran out in a teddy and put the thing back
in its cage. Marina That Bird Should Be
Put To Sleep. It's Miserable Marina, Look
At It. He's my baby, Marina snapped,
touching it through the cage's gold bars.
Don't you even think about killing him!
It's all we could think about, every whore
in the house had her own fantasy of giving its
wrecked neck a final twist, but no one did.

Marina really loved it.

No one knew that the whole time Marina was on a ton of coke. Or that she was moonlighting at another whorehouse right down the street, getting men from Lynn's house to see her there on the sly meaning she was fucking over Lynn, and they were friends. Lynn fired her of course, and Marina went away and then a couple days later there was a call from the rival whorehouse down the block—Marina had been passed out in one of the rooms for days, going in and out of consciousness, would Lynn come get her? Lynn would not. She passed the competing madam a number for Marina's police officer boyfriend. How could Lynn have known exactly how fucked up and desperate Marina was? She told her cop boyfriend that Lynn was to blame for her grand bottoming-out, that it was Lynn who had gotten her hooked her on cocaine, and Lynn who turned her out to pay for her habit.

It was a very beautifully dramatic made-for-tv-movie fabrication

 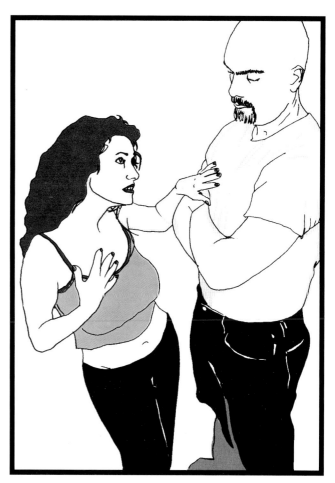

that the cop of course believed.

I mean, he had believed that Marina was a receptionist, answering the phone in her scandalously short clothing, boobs spilling out all over the place. The cop threatened to arrest Lynn who was, on the best of days, completely paranoid about getting arrested. So she shut everything down and no one had jobs and everyone was miserable. I signed on with an out-call agency but it was slow, and out-calls felt like giant pains in the ass as I was accustomed to the men coming to me. The nightly cab rides all over town, the weirdness of being in their space. When they came to our space, the men were nervous, out of their element, and left quickly lest the doors be kicked in by a vice squad accompanied by a Fox Television film crew. When we went to them, they kept us for the whole hour, comfortable and showy in their nice homes and apartments. I was spoiled.

Lynn rented a new space in an apartment building around the corner, just off Comm Ave., and all the girls had to help her move or else she'd fire us. We carried the fat, heavy furniture down the street at like five o'clock in the morning, because she was breaking her lease. We had to get all the stuff out before the building manager woke up. A few weeks into the new digs, Lynn's boyfriend Mark tried to kill her. I guess he was on a lot of drugs, too. All the girls were really freaked out about the attempted murder, having mistaken Mark for a nice guy, allowing him to hang around the house during working hours, privy to all our whorey secrets. He tried to strangle Lynn, left fingerprint bruises in a ring around her neck. She got a restraining order on him, and then he apologized for having tried to kill her so they got back together. Apparently he was really sorry.

Marina I don't know what happened to. She was so young, like nineteen, though she looked so much older with all the makeup

And truly, she loved her pigeon.

Body and Mind

Lynn had a call for me and she swore that it'd be easy. Lynn was full of shit.

Ever since she set me up with that seven hour coke call she'd been luring me to work—if not coming in to the house then hanging out at home awaiting out-calls—with promises of it happening again, keeping me by the phone, sending me out on other, less profitable calls that required me to actually work, until all my hope was killed. I knew that the call of my career had already happened, and the rest of my life as a prostitute would be spent yearning for what once was. I think he's gonna call tonight, Lynn would whisper, her voice full of promise. You want to sign on? She must have done it to me that night, I can't imagine why else I would've signed on in the middle of a blizzard. I don't know how the cab even made it down Steph's Jamaica Plain street, dead-ended and ignored by the snowplows. I always knew the cab drivers who were sent by Lynn to fetch me. She had a special deal with three or four of them, and I think I was riding with the Captain that night.

The Captain was a real piece of work.
You know, I was raped by a woman once, he rasped from the front seat.

Really? Yeah, she handcuffed me and she, she sat on it, and I kept telling her to stop and she wouldn't. I'm Sorry Captain, That's Terrible, I said. The Captain had sailed boats once, hence his name, but now he drove cabs and sold painkillers. He took me through the bleak winter landscape of February Boston, dead everything, a desert of snow. No one on the road but suckers like me. How come you're working tonight? he asked. Lynn tell you that druggie was gonna call? I harrumphed from the back seat. That guy hasn't called in a while, observed the Captain. He's Probably Dead, I said wistfully.

That night's call was at a hotel in I don't know, Boston or Cambridge. Everything looked different and foreign in the intense snow that blew down on the windshield like a biblical curse. The Captain parked the cab and ushered me through it. I hobbled in my heels, holding onto his arm like a bannister. It wasn't good weather for 'ho fashion, and I hated feeling helpless. The hotel was one of those motor lodges where you just went up to the door and knocked instead of having to parade yourself through the lobby like a circus animal.

Steph got a call at one of those places once, a fake one.

The boys at the desk had rung the agency as a joke, they wanted to see what a prostitute looked like. She looked like anyone, regular, long-haired girl, white, blue eyes that gleamed like little weapons, knife-eyes. Mean, mean Steph. I loved it when she was mean to tricks—the ones she tormented with phone calls, ratting their infidelities to blubbering wives, righteous cruelty, my Valerie Solanas. But feminist anger was not the actual root of Steph's wrath—the world was just lucky she'd found a cause to attach herself to. Steph was simply mean, and it could be turned on me, her hooker girlfriend, partner in crime, girl revolutionary, as easy as on any john.

The Captain deposited me at the hotel door and said he'd see me in an hour. Lynn had prepared me for this call.

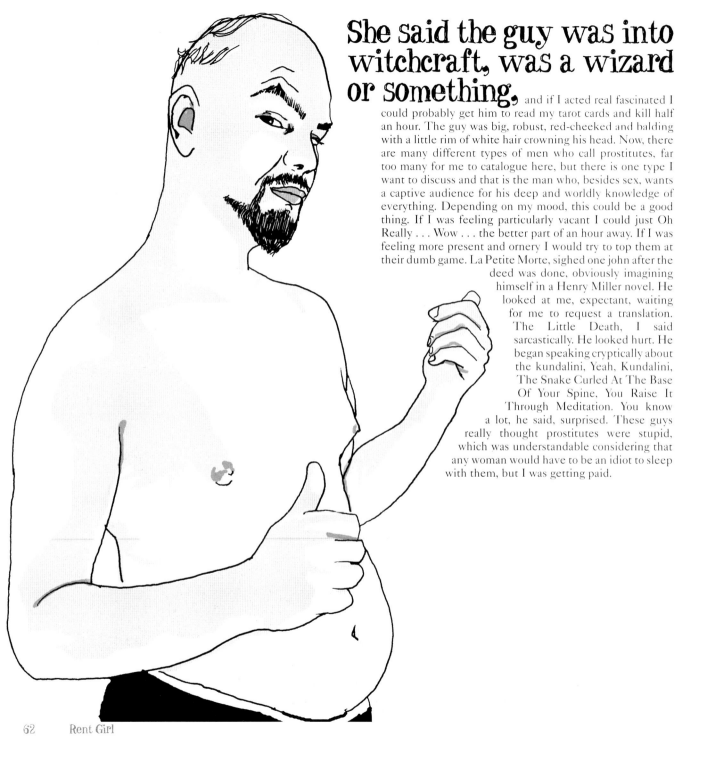

She said the guy was into witchcraft, was a wizard or something,

and if I acted real fascinated I could probably get him to read my tarot cards and kill half an hour. The guy was big, robust, red-cheeked and balding with a little rim of white hair crowning his head. Now, there are many different types of men who call prostitutes, far too many for me to catalogue here, but there is one type I want to discuss and that is the man who, besides sex, wants a captive audience for his deep and worldly knowledge of everything. Depending on my mood, this could be a good thing. If I was feeling particularly vacant I could just Oh Really . . . Wow . . . the better part of an hour away. If I was feeling more present and ornery I would try to top them at their dumb game. La Petite Morte, sighed one john after the deed was done, obviously imagining himself in a Henry Miller novel. He looked at me, expectant, waiting for me to request a translation. The Little Death, I said sarcastically. He looked hurt. He began speaking cryptically about the kundalini, Yeah, Kundalini, The Snake Curled At The Base Of Your Spine, You Raise It Through Meditation. You know a lot, he said, surprised. These guys really thought prostitutes were stupid, which was understandable considering that any woman would have to be an idiot to sleep with them, but I was getting paid.

Mr. Wizard had a little tin lamp resting on the hotel television, and he started in right away.

What do you see, he asked dramatically, holding out the object. Uh . . . It's A Lamp. How many sides does it have? Four. Do you know why it has four sides? It was just a regular, square fucking lamp, but I knew what he was getting at. The Four Directions, I said, North, South, East, West. The Four Elements, Earth, Air, Fire, Water. The Four Vulnerable Points On A Rapist's Body, Eyes, Knees, Groin, Throat. Mr. Wizard was clearly startled. These guys think they're Henry Higgins, dreaming of my transformation into a silk purse. You could see reels of Pretty Woman twirling in his head. Do you practice The Craft? he asked excitedly. I could tell the minute I saw you, your energy. Do you belong to a coven?

New age tricks were the worst.

They really thought they were doing something spiritual. No, No, I said, I Just Know Some Stuff. Hey, Do You Read Tarot Cards? Yes, yes, he rushed over to a chest of drawers and slid one open. But he pulled out a book instead, some men's movement thing about Thor or the Green Man. Have you read this? Excellent book. He started telling me about this really special, really sacred place in the woods where him and all his male friends go and hop fire and drum. That's Really Great, I said. I was bored. I didn't see tarot cards anywhere. What's your sign? he probed. Aquarius. Oh, yes, Aquarius, that's a very special sign. Yeah, I Know. Oh . . .the hour's getting away from us, he said, glancing at his watch.

That was the very worst call.

I need to tell you that I had an orgasm. It was awful. I felt it coming on like a sneeze and I couldn't believe it. Maybe some of you have had this experience.

First, let me explain the relationship I had with the enigmatic phenomena that is orgasm.

I had only just confessed to Steph that I'd been faking it all along. Steph, the laziest lover ever. After I got her off she would lie there like a big wet sea creature, some sluggish lump on the ocean floor. She would tug me into position above her mouth and halfheartedly snack at my pussy. I'd brace myself on the wall above our futon, thighs straining, and when it was clear that I was only going to end up cramped and exhausted I faked a gasping buck on her chin as if she was a trick, and sunk back down into bed with her. There were a few instances at the start of our relationship when things seemed promising. Once she bound my wrists behind my back with clothesline, but then Dinah came home all frenzied because the garbage men were outside and they hadn't brought the trash down. Steph just left me there in bed, door open so Dinah could understand how wild she was, a tied-up damsel left naked and panting on her futon while she hefted a weeks worth of garbage out into the street.

But really I knew it wasn't Steph's fault, not ultimately. It was something about my body, my body and my mind, a hard little computer that whirred and clanked like industry. Not even sex's rosy lushness could pull the plug. My body—a kind of briefcase to lug my mind around in.

In the privacy of my own bed, at night, before sleeping, alone with my thoughts, great. But not with another person.

So you can imagine my alarm at this toad between my legs, this situation I had no erotic connection to.

Like the malfunctioning machine that it was, my body was responding. His little gray head, pink bits of scalp, flanked by my skinny legs, traitor flesh. I had to make a decision. What an awful decision to have to make. I was going to fake it anyway, as part of my regular whore routine, so either way he was going to think he was a little champ, but I would know. I let it come on. Like most orgasms, it felt pretty good. He pulled himself off me. Oh, Tiffany, he said. I always have really wonderful energy with Aquarians.

I went into the bathroom and sat down on the cold hotel toilet.

I didn't choose for that to happen. But cosmically we choose everything, don't we. So on some intangible level I chose to have an orgasm with this creep. Why, to learn something? Learn what? That my body was even more Other than I had thought, something separate, something I was hopelessly stuck with, like a siamese twin. It made its own decisions and I shared the consequences. I looked at myself in the big, lit-up mirror above the sink. Scrawny white girl, little tits, boney arms, lipstick clinging dryly to the lips. Was I looking at me, or at my body.

Back in the room a pair of headlights shone in through the windows. I think your cab's here, said Mr. Earth Man. He watched me put my clothes on. You're going to find a coven, Tiffany. I can see you in a Dianic coven. But be careful, there's a lot of lesbians in those groups. They have no balance. You need the goddess AND the god. Out in the cab the Captain was smoking a cigarette. You got another one, he asked, or am I taking you home?

I'm Going Home, I said.

Steph was alone in bed when I pushed into our little warm room, heat blasting out the metal grate on the wall, an old, burnt smell. The lights were out and there was a ring of glass candles around the futon, the bobbing flames scorching the sides a charcoal black. She was sulking and listening to Ani DiFranco. I could tell she wanted to be alone, but there was nowhere for me to go. We lived together in this one room. Steph's body was on the bed. She was a Virgo. Always I think these things come back to that, astrology. Steph knew when to eat and what to feed her body, what was good for it. She massaged herself with the guts of a ripped stalk of aloe, or with oil jasmine-scented oil. She sat in the woods and was content just to be there, watching plants growing imperceptibly before her.

She knew how to take her Space, how to set Boundaries and be Alone,

and she could turn evil when it wasn't possible, when I broke her little ring of candles and reminded her that I lived in that room, too. Hi, I whispered, trying not to wreck the somber little church-vibe she had going. The Church of Steph. Hi, she muttered.

When I had confessed to Steph that I was faking all my orgasms I'd expected her to yell at me. Her fury was so unpredictable, and nothing brought it out like weakness. I'd expected to feel shamed and incompetent and less than lesbian. It was a shock to feel her twine her soft arms around me in the dark, her hand pulling my head to the hard bone of her sternum. It's all right, she breathed, I totally understand. Was I crying? Steph scared me.

It seemed we broke up daily, though nothing was ever said,

the situation never talked about, Processed. Just a disgusted glance as she entered the room we shared and saw me on the futon, tarot cards in a cryptic arc around me. A withering stare as I dumped morning granola into a dish, a violent shrug as I came up behind her and leaned my belly onto her back. I tried not to ruffle her mood. If we broke up I would have to leave, and right then I had nowhere to go.

Do You Want Some Time Alone? I asked her that night, Ani's warbling trill ringing out from the small radio on the floor. Um, please, she said sharply like I was dumb to have even asked. I wanted to tell her about the call, ask if her body had ever turned on her, but embarrassment lumped in my throat. I took a shower, stayed in there forever, so Steph could finish whatever she was doing in our room— lying around, being with herself. The water turned cold around me, freezing like the awful snow outside, like everything. When I returned to the room Ani was silent, the candles blown out and the air stinking of hot wax and smoke. Steph pretending to be asleep. I crawled in beside her, her body and mine.

Sleep crept in like a power outage, putting out the lights.

I Like To Give Women Pleasure

The man from Israel came for a two-girl call at the Comm Ave. whorehouse.

Let me tell you that the Comm Ave. whorehouse looked like a fake place on the inside, a place where people pretended to be living a certain life, sitting on the puffy black lease-to-own couch in the 'living room', or eating take-out from the Boston Chicken across the intersection at the glass-topped table in the 'kitchen.' On the clear kitchen tabletop would be my plastic spoon and my paper napkins and my tiny square packets of salt, pepper. The kitchen and the living room were one large room, undivided. At the smeary kitchen table I was spooning corn from Boston Chicken into my mouth.

Corn I knew was not vegan because the girl standing before the steaming trough of vegetables, when I asked her if there was butter in the corn she said Yeah! all bright, totally happy to be scooping me a styrofoam container of buttery corn. Until she saw my face sort of fall and sharply caught herself and went Uh-uh! I mean, no butter! I don't think. You Don't Think? I led the question hopefully. My stomach was all air and wind, a blustering storm in my middle, the intestinal weather knocking over telephone poles and whipping branches of trees into the street. My belly was a black hole, matter eating itself, folding inward with a groan that reached the ears of this black-haired girl who snapped a plastic cap onto my half-pint of buttery corn. You sure that's all? she asked, wrinkling up her nose the way grown-ups demonstrate concern to small children. She had heard the deep echoes of my rumbling stomach. She was a helper. I looked at her tag. DONNA, the white letters contrasted against the red pin above her heart. DONNA was really cute. My blood sugar was low, it flooded me with a manic euphoria edged in doom. DONNA's eyes were on me. Maybe DONNA thought I was cute, too. Maybe I was in love with DONNA. Any chicken today? she asked kindly. I shook my head, checked my takeaway bag for the necessary eating accessories, the napkin and spoon that I would not find in the vacant cabinets of the whorehouse—which, incidentally, we never called whorehouse, us females who worked there. We called it the in-call.

I decided to come back to the Boston Chicken once my blood sugar evened out and confirm the cuteness of DONNA.

We called it the in-call,

the place with the kitchen cupboards perpetually bare, the pretend-apartment. Once I thought of it as a movie set, a place we filled as actors. Really it was more like the fake offices flung up inside tall buildings where elaborate scams take place and people are bilked out of millions of dollars. Our building was not so tall, your average Boston brownstone crammed with low-rent college students, old women riding the elevators with their aluminum walkers, their pushcarts of groceries. And our scam was not so elaborate. There could have been other in-call operations tucked into our building, the women washing their laundry in the fluorescent -lit basement all whores, who knows. Not an elaborate scam, prostitution; a simple scam, ancient and famous.

Back to the layout of our illicit digs. My point about the kitchen was, even if you wished to be away from the smoke of a coworker, one who enjoyed the steady ignition of a chain of Marlboros while fixing her eyes to the magnetic glow of the endless television, even if you would have liked to eat your not-so-vegan corn in a less polluted environment, it would be too bad for you because the living room and kitchen were that one long, phony room and there was no escape. I could go into the bedroom to eat but come on—gross. The reek of swindle was strongest in the bedrooms.

I ate in the smoky kitchen with the empty cabinets. There was one little drawer that slid out from the counter, if you pulled it open you would find take-out menus and a gang load of cash. It's where we left Lynn's cut. After pleasantly escorting the john into the room—we're escorts, people, we escort—and sweetly requesting the wad of money which had been withdrawn from a teller or machine especially for me, I'd instruct him to make himself comfortable, and swish back out of the room. In the 'kitchen' I'd separate Lynn's cut from my small stack of money, toss it into the menu drawer. The rest got stuffed into my army bag.

On the days Lynn didn't come in, days and nights I was alone in the apartment, I kept it all for myself.

Being alone in the in-call with a trick was creepy enough to justify the small theft, I thought. I should get paid extra for having to endure the ringing lack of sound outside the bedroom; the understanding that, should screams erupt from my throat, they would call absolutely no one to my rescue.

When I returned to the room the john better be naked or else I'd have to assume he was a cop and thank god that never happened. What would I have done? Probably give him an hour-long back rub. Which would've involved a lot more physical energy then just lying back and being fucked. If I had the energy for physical labor I'd be at a real job in the first place, right? I didn't have a lot of energy for physical labor right then, what with my vegan diet and shitty attitude.

So the man from Israel—he called on an afternoon when I was there alone, all alone. Lynn was earning her business degree at BU and Babs was taking care of her kids out in Hull. Marina was long gone. Della wouldn't be in 'till her shift at the post office was over.

Della had one fucking work ethic.

Della was working hard so she wouldn't have to work anymore, a strategy I understood. That had been my idea too, but hooking isn't the cash call I thought it would be when I started. It was a good living for sure, especially if the alternative is working for seven bucks an hour, which it was, but it's not like you can buy yourself a house at the end of the year. Not at our place. Hours would go by without the phone ringing.

You could be the most eager, ready-to-work whore in the world and it didn't matter shit if the men weren't calling.

Steph, my beloved girlfriend, was nowhere to be found. She was lying at home stoned on pot or else shopping, spending the money she made the day before. Steph was lazy, she hardly ever worked. I thought it was perhaps because Steph was rich, and had parents who would be rich forever. I thought about this spoiled parental situation, thought about Steph at home, the morning lazily stretching into day the way her body stretched naked across the futon, the words I'm not working today coming out of her mouth on a breathy yawn. All I could do is work, work and work like some fairy-tale girl turning straw to gold by the ferocity of her labor. I had to work or I'd have nothing.

Dinah would be in later, to keep me company in the apartment that grew creepier as the sun dripped away outside the big windows. The TV illuminated the perpetual cloud of smoke, our atmosphere.

Nobody was there when I answered the phone and officially became three people.

First I was Bev, the phone girl. Bev didn't take calls, though the men tried like hell to set up dates with her. Bev would flattered when they tried, she acted like, though she worked at a whorehouse it had never, ever occurred to her to turn a trick herself. Bev would tell the men that such a thing was forbidden, and she would be fired—fired!—by the cruel madam if she was caught stealing calls from the girls. Being the first female voice a prospective trick encountered would give any girl an unfair advantage over the others, the lines of mute type and measurements lacking the dynamic personality of Bev's chirpy voice. The girls would kill me, Bev would explain to the men. They would slice her face with their long long nails, they would rip the tongue from her mouth and see if she got another job answering telephones in this town. I enjoyed creating dramatic soap opera excuses for the men. The place could use a cat fight every now and then, if you asked me. It was beyond boring. Bev—whose name was lifted from the cursive stitching above the breast of a recently thrifted work shirt—would be completely sweet about these guys trying to turn her into a prostitute when she was just trying to be a receptionist. Unless the man was particularly relentless, giving Bev the suspicion that he was just calling to fuck with the phone girl and not schedule an actual paying call with anyone. Then Bev would snap, I Don't Want To Fuck You. You Can't Afford Me. Would You Like To Book A Call With Someone You Can Afford? And the phone would click dead in my ear.

If the john was able to snap out of the spell of enchantment Bev's voice cast upon him—a real female voice! they got so attached, so quickly—he was allowed to choose between two girls, Allison and Tiffany. Both of them were me.

Allison was me regular, more or less.

Me with some makeup maybe, but not if I could slide by without it, not if Lynn was at school instead of chasing me through the hall with a pink-dusted brush. Allison was a college student, sort of quiet; she radiated a low contempt that seemed at odds with her smile. I think that it was the tension of these opposing forces—Allison's sincerely kind smile and her truly bad vibes—that kept the men coming back. There is no other explanation. She had no tits and didn't go out of her way to either look or act sexy. She came with hairy armpits, and if you removed her thigh-high tights you would know her hairy legs as well. Men inevitably asked Allison if she was a feminist and she would answer honestly, she would say Yes. If you were stupid enough to discuss feminism with a prostitute, Allison would go there. You would have to forget everything that came out of her mouth in order to enjoy it later on your cock. If you asked Allison if she was a lesbian, though, she would lie. She did not want tricks to imagine her having sex with another girl because she didn't want to sell out a sister like that, not without her consent, not even an imaginary one. Allison had a boyfriend, a real open-minded one, an artist, if the john needs to know. The john, if he'd made it this far, would inevitably comment on Allison's intellect, or her apparently bohemian lifestyle. The john would sound a bit surprised by the intellect, a bit envious of the bohemia, and a bit scared of them both. Allison had long black hair. She had measurements, a chain of numbers that didn't mean anything to me but were what Lynn told me to tell the callers. The numbers were listed in my ad in the Phoenix, a magic combination that unlocked the safe of men's wallets. Allison's measurements exaggerated a little. Allison's measurements rang falser each day, as my compassionate vegan diet hijacked what little tits I had to start, narrowed my hips, flattened my ass.

Tiffany was me with a big blond wig and a slightly better attitude.

Tiffany smiled a good deal more, a toothy happy-to-see-ya smile. If Tiffany's smile was a state it would be Texas. Tiffany was, I imagined, very Texas. Not that I'd ever been there. Tiffany was a joke, a giant caricature. Her measurements were even larger then Allison's lying stats, hilarious. Tiffany would toss on a little lipstick, Tiffany went the extra mile. Tiffany was not a feminist—Tiffany had no idea how that hair got in her armpits! Tiffany was so embarrassed! She totally forgot to shave! Tiffany went to college—they all went to college, it's the only way to excuse this prostituting behavior plus it's practically a fucking tax write-off for the men, a donation toward tuition with a complimentary blowjob—but, Tiffany wasn't sure what her major was. Allison was more like me but I always preferred being Tiffany. I liked to do the least amount of work possible, and I found it was more work being myself, easier to let my personality float away on some current, airborne. I became buoyant with Tiffany. Her only major drawback was her wig and its hot itch, the way her hairline tended to shift as she crawled across the bed.

The man from Israel wanted girl on girl action.

After a brief attempt to turn out Bev the phone girl, he asked for a double call with Allison and Tiffany. He wanted to watch them kiss each other with showoff tongues. He wanted their tongues to have the shape and texture of strawberries, he wanted them to nuzzle, to spar gently like baby rams. I wished someone was in the apartment with me, to witness the hilarity of me trying to get out of doing a two-girl call with myself, but that's the point, no one was there but the me and my ghostly trinity. Oh, Allison And Tiffany Don't Do Calls Together, I said. But you said they did, he corrected me. Oh, Well, They Do Girl-On-Girl Calls, Just Not With Each Other, I told him. I lowered my voice— Bev's voice—into a gossipy whisper. They Don't Like Each Other Very Much. No? he asked. No, I confirmed. I thought about it, briefly—yeah, Allison and Tiffany really wouldn't like each other. Tiffany was exactly the kind of female Allison perceived herself locked in philosophical battle with. Tiffany would think Allison frighteningly unfeminine, would worry about the implications of such a lack of femininity. They don't have to touch each other, the man from Israel adjusted his fantasy to fit these new limitations. They can both touch me. No, I said sternly. They Can't Even Be In The Same Room Together, I whispered. They Really, Really Hate Each Other.

Who is better, Allison or Tiffany? Oh, It Depends What You Like, I said breezily. I just couldn't play favorites with myself. Sure, Tiffany was more cake for me, but I couldn't bring myself to encourage the guy to choose the blond bimbo over the angry, sullen feminist. I didn't want these guys to have a good time. The man from Israel wanted Allison, but he just couldn't let go of his two-girl fantasy. Would Bev do a call with Allison? That's Disgusting, Bev scolded. Bev is sometimes a raging bulldagger, sometimes rabidly homophobic. It all depends on the desire I'm trying to extinguish. When will a playmate for Alison arrive? There was Dinah in later. I liked Dinah a lot. We both had the same sort of low self-esteem that allowed for close relationships with people like Steph. What was Dinah's whore name, I shuffled through the ad clippings in the three-ring binder. Veronica Comes In At Eight, Bev purred into the receiver. You Can Have A Session With Them At Eight O'Clock.

Poor Dinah had barely a second to breathe.

The minute her key let her into the place she had to shuck her slovenly jeans and sack-like t-shirt. Dinah was impossibly tall and I think what is called 'willowy.' She was languid. She actually looked like an actual model. All that height, and the sharp cheekbones her vegan diet has accentuated. Her eyes were that prized blue color, her nose sort of big but in a way that was decidedly European. It added to her model-ness, and made her look haughty and intimidating, a decent mask for her nervous passivity. Dinah's hair was long and always dirty, but again, it looked deliberate, like very clean hair that had been spritzed with a product designed to make cared-for hair look unkempt. Dinah looked like a junkie whose habit was on the verge of becoming a problem, but is still just the tiniest bit exciting. Really she was just a sloppy vegan. She had some sort of musky-smelling soup in a plastic container and she was dying to eat it. I imagined the combined rumbling of our stomachs overwhelming our faked shrieks of passion. By the time our call was done Dinah's soup would be cool, the surface clotted with vegetable muck.

She pulled stockings onto her endless legs and clamped them to the garters that dangled from her corset.

She looked like a spider. A little makeup made Dinah look incredible, like a magazine. A little makeup worked to make me look more convincingly heterosexual. I was hoping that I wouldn't actually have to suck face with or otherwise interact with Dinah, as she was my friend and roommate and it would just be weird. It would be weird enough, I knew, to watch her get fucked or give head or whatever would be expected of us. I couldn't bear the thought of having to touch her boobs or something. Luckily, Dinah had better boundaries then me. No, we don't do anything together, she said simply. No offense. She winked at me. Really? I asked. We Can Just Say No? I just figured, a two-girl call and you'd have to lez out for them. Don't worry, she said, and slipped a tight dress over her head, pulled her stringy hair from under the collar. Dinah's mouth was just like Mick Jagger's. Maybe that was it, the crux of her beauty, a mouth so wide.

In the fake kitchen me and Dinah, who is now Veronica, divided up the dollars.

In the balance hung Lynn's cut, about a hundred. Fuck her, Dinah decided. We split it, dawdled so that the man from Israel had adequate time to "get comfortable." He was good-looking in a bland way, as all men were. I mean, they just didn't move me. Probably he'd move someone else. Do You Think He's Cute? I asked Dinah. Dinah was straight. She probably still is. She shrugged. I guess. No one cute ever came into the in-call, cute wasn't a relevant category. They were either gross or not-gross.

The guy from Israel wasn't gross.

He was clean, his thick dark hair was groomed, his face shaved soft. He had wide shoulders, was sort of big. His clothes, when we reentered the bedroom, were folded into a neat pile on the chair. He had his tighty whities on. He sat in the middle of the bed with his arms outstretched, marking the spaces we were meant to fill, a girl tucked beneath each arm. Come, girls, he boomed. He was happy. He talked to us. He'd been in the Israeli army, he just got out. He DJ'd a radio show on Sunday mornings, all Israeli music. He asked us nothing about ourselves, it's how we all liked it. Dinah and me were like a couple of bobble-headed dashboard toys, heads waggling in unison to the beat of his talk. Heads nodding on our skinny vegan necks. Oh. Wow. Oh, Wow. Lots of smiles.

The man from Israel was one of those guys who like to give women pleasure.

They always said it like that, the grossest possible phrase: I like to give women pleasure. Lucky Dinah got her pleasure first. She lied on her back and he put his face between her legs. It must suck to be Dinah, I thought. It must suck to have there be so little to distinguish your tricks from the people you actually dated. From what I could see, the only thing that kept the bike-messenger types Dinah went out with from being johns was their inability to pay for it.

I spaced out to the soft rock that streamed from the clock radio on the bedside table. That radio station always played Sting and always I will resent him for being the soundtrack to my sex work. Always will Sting be the musical equivalent of the gruesome phrase I Like To Give Women Pleasure. I was losing myself in the mind-numbing groove when Dinah faked her orgasm. It was a good one. A little dramatic, but that's what they pay for. Not too dramatic. The guy pulled himself up on his elbows and glowed proudly at Dinah, awaiting his compliment. You should do that professionally, she gushed, and shot me a fast look.

Now you, he commanded. I lied back on the pillows and prepared to endure my pleasure. It was almost painful, the terrible annoyance of his face probing my parts. I faked my orgasm quickly. A little louder then Dinah, a little showier. I did it to entertain her. She looked so bored, her eyes cast away to give me privacy. They seemed glazed. That Wildfire song from the seventies crooned out from the cheap radio. My big phony orgasm perked Dinah up, she looked at me and our eyes locked. Oh Yeah! I moaned like a porn star and she spit out a laugh, slapped her hands to her giant mouth to hold in the rest. You again? dude turned to Dinah.

Women can take so much pleasure!

Dinah's next orgasm was almost ridiculous.

She sounded like some gigantic woman-bird, cawing. Caw, caw! Dinah shrieked from the bed. How to top her without exposing it for the competitive charade that it was? I remembered a call Steph had told me about, how she'd squeezed a palmful of K-Y jelly from the tube and slicked it to her crotch right there on the bed, in front of her guy. He'd brought his hand over to her artificial wetness and cooed, You're so wet. Yeah, I Just Put Some K-Y Down There. Remember? Steph snapped. You must be really turned on, the guy continued, as if she hadn't spoken. He thinks K-Y's a fucking aphrodisiac! she later fumed. Stupid people made Steph very angry. I thought that her expectations of humanity must have been very high. It was proof of her idealism, that she was so constantly let down. Her anger, I decided, was simply the measure of her hope.

I thought about the john believing that the thick goop between Steph's legs was liquid evidence of the incredible lust he'd inspired and decided I could totally beat Dinah's orgasm.

I got into position, my legs framing his head.

Oh how my knees would have loved to box his ears. A quick snap, oooh. The hard part was building my final and most absurd climax. For it to be really insane it would have to build, and the longer it builds the longer I suffer. My cries sounded pained because they were. About to let it rip, I looked at Dinah, her eyes wide and incredulous she was just laughing, openly, because my howls drowned her out and the man was safely attached to my snatch like some sort of terrible parasite, oblivious. I thrashed around on the pillows. Oh! I screamed. Oh! Oh! Oh! Oh, David! I screamed the name he had given us. Do the men feel ripped off, I wondered, when at the frenzied height of our phony pleasure we scream a name not theirs. Do they feel a rush of regret, do they bite back the urge to blurt, It's Walter, actually, will you do it again and scream Walter this time?

David came to see me again.

Just me, Allison, without Dinah. It was only the luck of the draw that the initial call had ended on my extravagant imitation, making me the winner because there was no time left for Dinah to top me. When David came again he told me he didn't want to touch me. Not in a sexual way. He told me that he loved me for real and that he wanted to marry me and if he had to come and see me every week for a year, always paying me and never having sex, if that's what he had to do to prove his love, then that's what he would do. I felt a quick thrill at the idea of this, the perfect regular. Once a week! No sex! But johns like that seemed like time bombs to me. What happened when, at the end of the year, I didn't pay off? A chair through the bedroom window? A chair across my head?

David rubbed my shoulders through the crinkly fabric of the dress I wore, Steph's. Some black and white pattern, it fluttered on my scrawny frame. Steph had a real body—tits, hips, the works. Everyone seemed to be working out okay with the vegan diet, even Dinah's skinniness looked fairly natural. Only I was wasting away. David rustled through the dress till he found my tense shoulders, he rubbed them for an hour. After a while I forgot it was David rubbing me and felt only rubbed. Rubbed by a pair of magical, disembodied hands, rubbed by god. I love you, Allison, David told me at the door that released him to the dim hallway. Did you listen to my radio show? It's So Early, I said. You should listen, he said. I dedicate songs to you. Okay, I nodded. Between the deep massage and my low blood sugar I was barely there at all. I'll see you soon, David said, but he never came back. You should've heard Michelle's orgasm! Dinah said to Steph, cracking up. It was hilarious!

She totally won.

Crabby

When we came back to Boston that summer we moved into a one-room apartment in Provincetown, at the edge of Cape Cod.

You couldn't really call an apartment, it was just a room and I've told you about it before, but never this story. I had crabs in my crotch. Pubic lice, down in my hair there. They didn't really itch. I was sitting on the toilet in the afternoon, the communal bathroom on the second floor that you had to share with everyone else in the house—

the straight kids who drank and worked too much,

the conservative gay guy with the even tan,

the bleach-blonde dyke who worked at the leather store.

The quiet girl on the first floor with the boyfriend who stalked her,

who came into our house after the bars let out and banged on her door with the cast his broken arm was wrapped up in until one of the boys woke up and went down to talk to him down. And the stalker would start crying really loud, just blubbering, half-yelling stuff through his wet mouth, thick tongue, and somebody else would wake up and go across the street to the pay phone in the parking lot and finally call the cops. This happened all the time. The cops would gently escort him out of our house.

Me and Steph listened to the whole thing from our futon and grumbled, Jesus Christ. Talked a little about how much we hated men, went back to sleep.

But the bathroom, it was actually pretty clean considering how many people used it. I was sitting there peeing, and when I saw it I thought it was just a fleck of nature, like a bit of seaweed from being in the ocean, or sand. And I looked at it and I picked at it, it seemed to stick to me, and I noticed it had legs. Tiny ones poking out from it's side like a crab. I made a swift connection between my pubic hair and this thing that actually really looked like a little fucking crab, and I screamed, Steph! She was upstairs hitting the bong. She said she knew right when she heard me scream like that that I had crabs. She came thump thump thump down the stairs then rattle rattle at the bathroom door. I hopped off the toilet and waddled over with my underwear looped around my knees and pee dripping down my thighs, I unlatched the door and it felt like the dirtiest moment in the world. I started crying like crazy, greeting Steph there at the threshold of my nightmare, dripping from my face and crotch. I gulped, I Think I Have Crabs, and she said get in there, and pushed me back into the little room. The temple of hygiene with its many faucets and soaps and foaming bottles.

Steph locked the door and I plopped back on the bowl.

I hadn't really had many moral twinges about me and Steph's prostitution, none of the failing self-esteem and self-worth that were supposed to accompany a girl into such a profession. It was too easy.

I would look into the mirror and think, I Am A Prostitute, and wait for an appropriate wave of horror and revulsion.

I would wait and wait and feel nothing, and I'd wash my face and go back upstairs.

And now it was like all the pangs of guilt and conscience I never had took the form of parasitic bugs and burst forth from my crotch. That's what you get, I thought. Steph crouched by the bowl and poked around at me, pinched a small monster out with her fingertips. Yup, you have crabs.

Steph, I sobbed, They Really Look Just Like Little Crabs!

She hiked up her hippie dress and brought her pantiless crotch over to my face.

Do you see anything do you see anything? I searched through her hair like my mother checking my head for nits in kindergarten. I remember she had a certain comb for it, white plastic, and how poisonous the shampoo smelled—Kwell, a word that sounds like a bug. The whole neighborhood and extended family had gathered in my kitchen for the big soap, my head bent into the sink, suffocating beneath the shampoo fumes and water. My grandparents were there, it was a real big deal. Afterwards all the adults sat around drinking tea and chain-smoking, speculating on which filthy child could have passed me the bugs. They jump, my grandmother kept saying. I imagined them with small and powerful legs, big as the magnified picture that came with the shampoo instructions. Soap and water don't cost nothing, my mother clucked, disgust in her voice. Soap Costs, I protested, sticking my long wet hair into my nose, breathing the awful stink of it. Anyone can afford soap, my mother insisted. It doesn't cost anything to be clean. They went on about who let their kids run around wild and how Chelsea was going to hell. It was all about dirt in this really moral, really virtuous way, and it was what I sat with trapped in the bathroom in Provincetown as Steph ran down to Adam's Pharmacy to buy razors.

What else did I know about lice, about crabs. They were evidence of betrayal.

After my parents divorced but before my father disappeared we were attempting to have a very 80s divorced family, a visit dad on the weekends situation, but Dad was such a jerk—a couple cans of Miller from the fridge and he'd start trying to pry information out of us: who was our mother's boyfriend, did he sleep over, did he buy her the car he'd seen her driving, a powder-blue Escort with a hatchback and who said I could go to Chelsea High and not Pope John or Saint Rose, why wasn't that discussed with him, he was my father—did I discuss it with my mother's boyfriend? And my breathing got all funny and I noticed the faster I breathed the funnier I felt, in my head, and it was like when I forgot to eat in the summer and then went out riding my bike until I saw spots in front of my eyes and fell over. I figured if I kept breathing faster and funnier I'd pass out and my dad would have to leave me alone. Jesus Christ, he sounded annoyed. Through my fuzzy eyes I could see my sister looking panicked and I wished she would get it and faint with me and then we could go home and Dad would be the big asshole for bothering his daughters until they were sick with it. I feigned unconsciousness for a few minutes. I was sprawled on that weird piece of furniture, Dad's first bachelor pad acquisition. Sort of a couch but long like a bed and covered in long orange fake fur. It looked a bit like a sports car. I 'came to,' and he called us a cab.

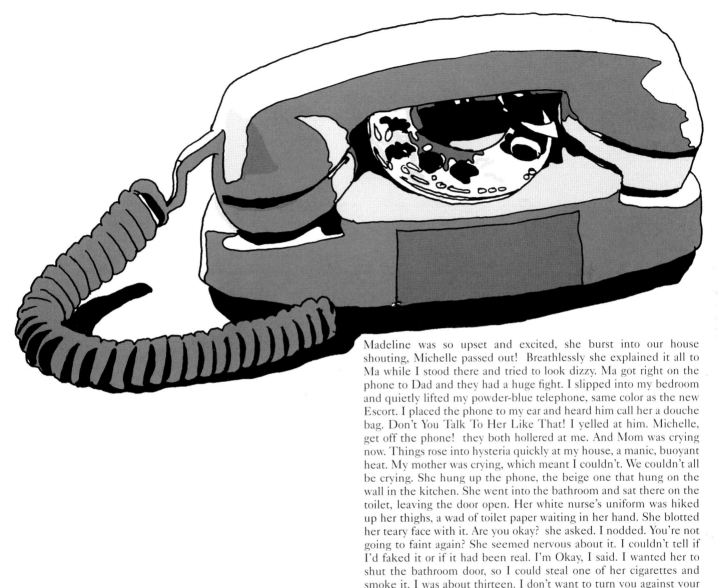

Madeline was so upset and excited, she burst into our house shouting, Michelle passed out! Breathlessly she explained it all to Ma while I stood there and tried to look dizzy. Ma got right on the phone to Dad and they had a huge fight. I slipped into my bedroom and quietly lifted my powder-blue telephone, same color as the new Escort. I placed the phone to my ear and heard him call her a douche bag. Don't You Talk To Her Like That! I yelled at him. Michelle, get off the phone! they both hollered at me. And Mom was crying now. Things rose into hysteria quickly at my house, a manic, buoyant heat. My mother was crying, which meant I couldn't. We couldn't all be crying. She hung up the phone, the beige one that hung on the wall in the kitchen. She went into the bathroom and sat there on the toilet, leaving the door open. Her white nurse's uniform was hiked up her thighs, a wad of toilet paper waiting in her hand. She blotted her teary face with it. Are you okay? she asked. I nodded. You're not going to faint again? She seemed nervous about it. I couldn't tell if I'd faked it or if it had been real. I'm Okay, I said. I wanted her to shut the bathroom door, so I could steal one of her cigarettes and smoke it. I was about thirteen. I don't want to turn you against your father, she said, which meant she was about to tell me something good. I'll tell you everything that happened when you're older. My father would say that too: wait 'til you're eighteen. Then a tight drag off his cigarette.

My mother was talking. I don't want to talk badly about him, he's still your father, she stalled. Ma It's Okay, I Don't Even Like Him. It was true. My Dad was rapidly becoming the biggest jerk in the world. It was hard to forgive him for kicking us all out of our house, hard to visit him and see the room that used to be mine, empty now but for a few cardboard boxes. A half-assed storage space. In his living room I'd watched MTV on the color television. We were watching a miniscule black-and-white job back at our new place, me Ma and Madeline. A small screen of static. Dad had cable. There was Mick Jagger, walking his weird turkey-walk through some inner city neighborhood. I ain't waiting on a lady, he sang. I'm just waiting on a friend.

That's my song, Dad said bitterly, his words coming out on a cloud of exhaled Vantage. Not waiting for a lady. I jumped inside. It scared me then, the contempt in his voice when he said 'lady,' the lift of the beer can to his wide, Polish mouth. Now I'm struck by his ability to be moved by a rock song, that he was listening hard

enough to hear the lyrics through the nasal British accent, that he related. The song comforted him in his evil, alcoholic mood. He was standing behind the bar he'd bought when Ma convinced him that we should at least have the living room furniture. We got the scratchy floral couch and the rickety armchair. He replaced it with a bar and the weird fluffy sofa-bed-thing. On the bar sat a box of Andes mints, the only food in the house. Later we'd go out for a bucket of Kentucky Fried Chicken and eat it on the floor in front of the television. For now I sucked on the cool, minty chocolates.

It was the last time we visited Dad.

When you kids were little he gave me crabs. He said that I gave them to him. Ma was really crying now, wiping at her cheeks with the toilet paper. I was always faithful to him, she said, and I believe her. She gulped and sobbed. Probably she never got to really cry about it. Don't you ever spread your legs for anybody! she yelled. Not angrily, just to get her point across. I nodded, slipped a cigarette slyly from her pack.

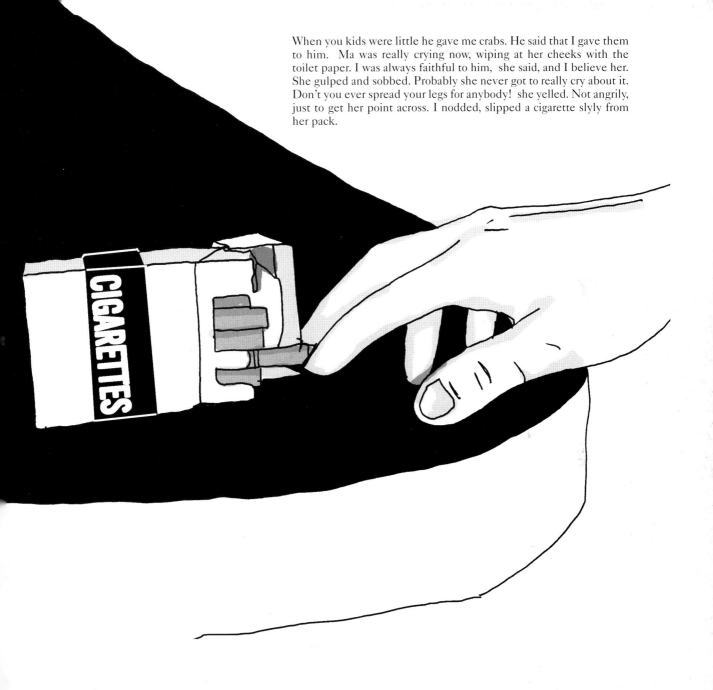

Steph came back to the bathroom and she had a little paper bag. It had plastic razors in it. Pink for girls, and also a can of girl-scented shaving cream—a pearly pink gel that lathered into a soapy paste. Oh God! I cried more, looking at the stuff. I just wanted something to come and make the crabs be gone. Make them never have been there. I'm going to shave too, Steph said. Steph was such a martyr. There weren't any bugs in her crotch. I could never have a tragedy of my own, she was always trying to one-up me. I could have eggs, she insisted. We tried to remember if we'd seen any of the same tricks. We slept in the same bed but we never had sex anymore.

I'm sure she didn't have the crabs.

We crowded naked into the shower,

which was like an aluminum closet. There was barely room for us both. To get at the tricky places we had to stretch our legs out onto the bathroom floor, getting the whole place wet. Steph was scared of the razor, but I understood you couldn't just lop your clit off the way she feared. Zzzt, zzzt zzzt, I brought the razor down over my pubic bone, instantly clogging it with thick curls I dug from the metal and flung into the drain. I hated Steph for blubbering. You really couldn't have something shitty happen to you without her stealing all the glory. I just wanted to die thinking about those gross things latched onto my skin with their little teeth, drinking my blood.

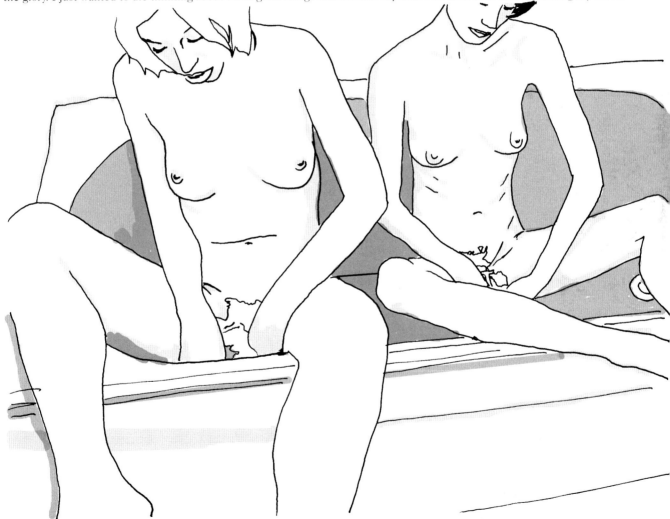

I Quit, I said to Steph, I'm Not Going To Whore Anymore.

I'm not quitting, Steph snapped, getting all tough on me. She plunged the razor bravely into her wet hair. They're just bugs. Right. It would all be another battle scar for Steph, one more way for her to lord it over the rest of the world who would never know hardship the way she had known hardship. She tossed a soggy mat of hair to the floor and squirted more shaving gel into her palm. She bent down to inspect my work. You got to get all of it, she said, pointing to the stubble. That's where the eggs are. I lathered up and scraped some more. My skin was raw beneath the metal. No, you really got to get rid of it, she said when my razor brought away nothing. Can't We Just Get Kwell? I pleaded. I was starting to whimper. Do you know how toxic that is! Steph snapped. That shit's poison, it's insecticide! Here, she took her razor, dug it into my skin. Steph! You have to shave it clean, she said. Little beads of blood formed on my pores. Lift your leg, she ducked beneath me to get in the folds of my labia, scrape, scrape. I spread my butt cheeks and she angled the thing around my anus. It was like she was shaving the skin away. Steph You Can't, I cried. It Just Hurts Too Much. If we don't get it now we'll have to do it all over again, she said simply. Steph was a virgo. Do me, she said once my entire genital area was shorn and burning. It looked like a hunk of chicken lying in the meat case. When we were through we took toilet paper and wiped up the mounds of hair that clogged the drain, the tiny drowning crabs. The paper melted in my hand as I flung the awful mess into the toilet.

Upstairs in our small, airless room we tried to find clothes that hadn't been worn since our last laundry.

I had a yellow skirt, long and flowing, that crepey, hippie material. Everything else got stuffed into trash bags. We stripped the futon. There were no laundromats in Provincetown, something about the water level or the ecosystem. Normally we brought our laundry into Boston and washed it in the laundry room in the brothel, but Steph wasn't due to work again for another work, and I had quit. You're not really going to quit, Steph said cynically, like I was talking about smoking. We brought our trashbags of contaminated laundry over to the town's wash and fold, to be shipped out and returned clean in three days. Make sure to use hot water, Steph said to the lady, and she smiled a queasy little smile at us.

Of course Steph turned the whole infestation into a giant excuse to go shopping.

We needed underwear, silk underwear that would feel nice against her burning cooch. We walked into the expensive lingerie store on Commercial Street with the salesladies who always looked like they wanted to kick us out. Every time I took a step my crotch stung like a hive of bees. Steph dropped a hundred bucks on a bunch of drawers. We deserve it, she said. A soft pile on the counter, all different colors, the coolest, most tender material. Next Steph needed coconut oil, a dense jar of it, to smear on her traumatized labia. Then we needed to have an expensive dinner at the pricey Italian restaurant, way down where Commercial Street got quiet and pretty. We ate homemade sorbet, lemon and orange, served in the hollowed-out skins of the appropriate fruit.

VICTORIA'S SECRET

That night we laid on our futon beneath atop a single clean sheet.

Steph slid her hands beneath her new silk underwear and smeared her cunt with coconut. I did the same. It did make it feel better. I'm going to masturbate, Steph announced. It seemed strange to just lie there uninvolved while this was happening, so I said Me Too, and rubbed the stinky oil around my clit. You don't have to, Steph said, annoyed. She always thought I was jumping her train.

In the morning we lay naked at the beach, in a tiny forest of sea grass.

Every time a sand flea hopped on my body I jumped. Steph had picked up a magnifying glass at the drugstore, she held it up to my irritated pussy and she found an egg, a single fucking egg like the tiniest glass bubble, stuck to a piece of stubble up by my butt hole. No! I wailed, and burst into tears again. Some fags passed by and looked at us curiously. We have to get rid of it, she said. Steph, I Can't Go Through That Again! I Want Kwell. At the pay phone in the parking lot we dialed 1-800-ASK-A-NURSE. The nurse said we needed Kwell. What if we shaved the area? Steph suggested, and the nurse said no, no, you need to shampoo. You're just a pawn of western medicine! Steph slammed the phone. The Active Ingredient In Kwell Is Flower Extract, I suggested hopefully. *It's poison!*

Inside our house the other tenants looked embarrassed when they saw us in the hallway. Certainly they knew we had crabs. Steph lathered up my ass again and raked the raw skin and it was the worst feeling you could imagine. There Can't Be Anything Left! I cried. Would Steph torture me? Was she that evil? She took the magnifying glass and inspected me deeply, promised that this time I was ok. We threw away the newly contaminated underwear and bought another pile, **went out to dinner at a seafood shack and ordered up a bunch of crab.**

A Working Vacation in Tucson

This was the best idea that I never did.

Steph and I went to Tucson, to visit her best friend Brad, another hustler. Apparently all a person needs to do is meet a prostitute and they will become one. Everyone Steph touched turned to 'ho. Brad hooked us up with his outcall agency, a joint that supplied both men and women to the lonely and moneyed of Tucson, and we hunkered down in the adobe he shared with his roommate Tulip, a long-haired, voluptuous Leo, part soulful hippie, part bluntly cynical New York Jew.

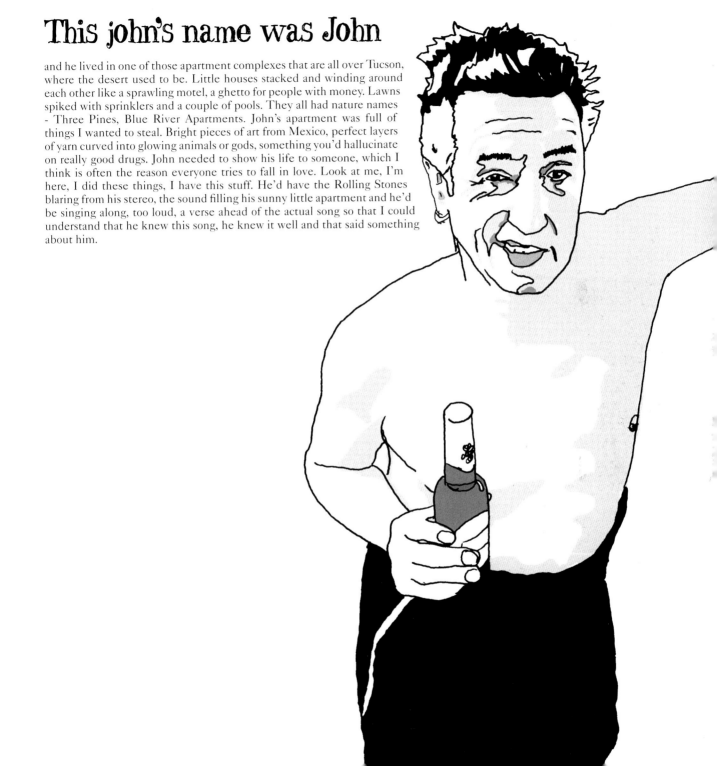

This john's name was John

and he lived in one of those apartment complexes that are all over Tucson, where the desert used to be. Little houses stacked and winding around each other like a sprawling motel, a ghetto for people with money. Lawns spiked with sprinklers and a couple of pools. They all had nature names - Three Pines, Blue River Apartments. John's apartment was full of things I wanted to steal. Bright pieces of art from Mexico, perfect layers of yarn curved into glowing animals or gods, something you'd hallucinate on really good drugs. John needed to show his life to someone, which I think is often the reason everyone tries to fall in love. Look at me, I'm here, I did these things, I have this stuff. He'd have the Rolling Stones blaring from his stereo, the sound filling his sunny little apartment and he'd be singing along, too loud, a verse ahead of the actual song so that I could understand that he knew this song, he knew it well and that said something about him.

The first thing I'd do when I got there was shower.

He would be freshly showered, wearing one of those terry cloth towels with a velcro bit that fastened around his waist. He'd have beads around his neck, and once he had sunglasses on. I think he was trying to cultivate a tropical resort-type atmosphere, so I'd have to be damp in a fluffy robe, smoking a cigarette, carefree. John would talk a lot about his family, who were very wealthy. He was the black sheep, misunderstood, the rebel. He would go on family vacations and hang out with his mom and his sisters while all the men talked about things he didn't care about, the family business. They sold welding equipment or something, and like the rest of the sons John had been recruited into this.

I'd get to his house and he'd be hunched over papers on a ton of cocaine,

adding and subtracting, cursing, sweating in his towel, dipping into the bathroom for more drugs I'm sure then sitting back at the papers with panic on his face. I'd read National Geographic, he had stacks of them. I read about dinosaurs and Antarctica and countries with huge and crumbling castles that people still lived in. Knowing there were so many places in the world I could go made it easier to be at John's house. Reggae loud on the stereo and he'd hand me a beer. Lime flavored Tostitos on the counter, *help yourself.*

It was so surreal.

I puttered around the kitchen in this teal bathrobe embroidered with the insignia of whatever expensive hotel the last family vacation took place at. I made espresso, he burned the rind of a lemon with a match. He was pretending he had a girlfriend. I was like the mannequins placed in those balsa wood houses they blew up in Nevada.

John had spent a summer on Cape Cod years ago,

an incredibly special, beautiful summer that I guess was the end of his youth or something. He talked about it on every visit, about his old friends, free spirits who were artists and musicians and continued to blow in the wind and not get roped into a family business. Many magical things had happened to John that summer. He found a little girl's jelly shoe at the shore and he knew that it meant something. It was sacred, Cinderella's shoe, and he placed it on the sand with great ceremony and drew a heart around it with a stick. The next day in that very spot on the beach lied the most beautiful woman he had ever seen, wearing a pair of jelly shoes. They were soul mates, he knew this immediately but nothing ever happened and so he was haunted by the memory. He was pathetic, moaning over a fleeting moment that had given him a glimpse of what it would be like to have a life, this wild romantic summer that was gone forever so now he called prostitutes and strutted around his apartment in sandals and sunglasses, trying to get the feeling back.

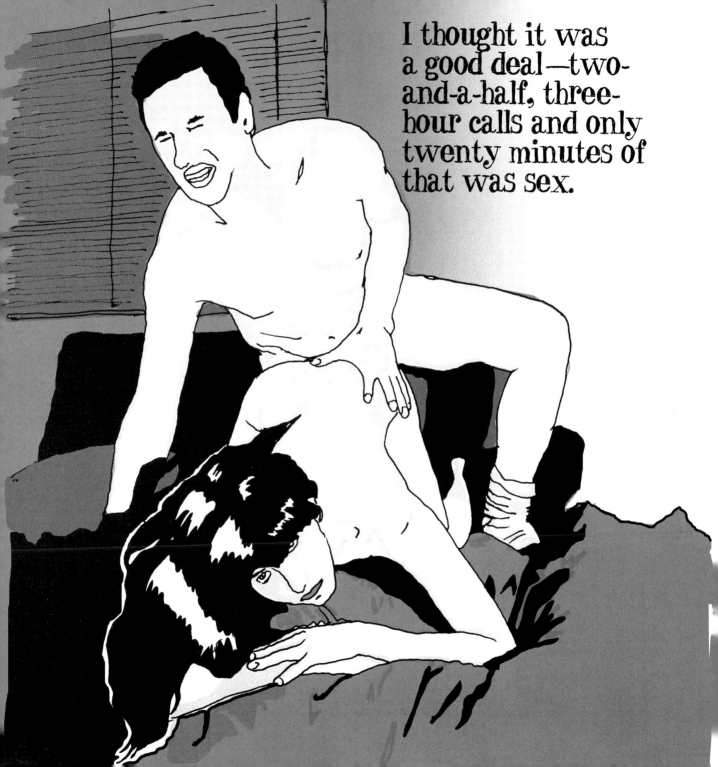

I thought it was a good deal—two-and-a-half, three-hour calls and only twenty minutes of that was sex.

The rest was leafing through National Geographic - or engaging John, keeping him talking the way I've always thought I would try to hold off a serial killer if something like that ever happened to me. But the thing about regulars, the really creepy thing is that if you see anybody often enough you're having a relationship with them. They become familiar, a character in your life in the impersonal way maybe a neighbor is, except you're fucking him, and he is repeating the history and epic myth of who he is over and over. With every visit he becomes more present in your life but still he doesn't fully exist, he can't. Like an imaginary friend you don't want.

I wanted to beat up and rob John, but the most I got to do was humiliate him.

It would have been so easy.

He had those Greenpeace stickers all over his walls, the National Geographics, he was really down with the environmental cause. I could give Steph a clipboard and some, you know, flyers and tree pictures. Brad was charming and blond, he could go with her. They were both blonde and their eyes were blue, they had tans, they looked exactly like the kind of liberal college students who did door canvassing for spending money.

John would let them right in, he'd be thrilled to have two new people to demonstrate his existence to, he'd probably even get them high and wham! —Steph could have a pipe or something tucked into her Guatemalan sack and just bash him in the face with it, knock him out, ransack his apartment, and I could get all the Mexican art that I deserved more than he did. A great plan. Steph always talked about different ways we could maim and kill our tricks, and I would point out the problems with her plans and she'd get bitchy and indignant, as if it were small minds like mine holding back the revolution. And then I come up with the ultimate strategy and she just acted like I'd lost my mind.

I'm not going to do THAT, she huffed. Are you CRAZY? So instead I taped John singing.

John had an acoustic guitar and all these songs he'd written himself.

Really terrible songs he sang in this rock starry voice that was a mix of different accents he didn't have.

He would sing them for me, and later, at Brad's on the couch with a glass of Mescal, I would sing them for everyone and everyone would crack up. It was so stupid and so pathetic and so hilarious. I needed to somehow tape-record it, so they could hear it for themselves. It was hard for me to convince John that this was ok. He was pretty paranoid, probably from the cocaine, and he was nervous that I would play these terrible folk recordings to other people, and that they would go and record them and cut a record and become famous rock stars, which was what John was planning on doing, eventually. I Just Love Those Songs, I said wistfully to John the john, I Have Them In My Head When I'm Hanging Out At Home, And It Would Be So Cool To Be Able To Listen To Them . . . I had always been a very nice, very compassionate person, and it was a sharp, exhilarating experience to indulge in such unbridled cruelty. Like punching my fist through a sheet of ice, a bloody chime.

Me and John sat on his couch in our terry cloth outfits, him with his guitar, me clutching my little tape recorder, angling the microphone part towards his mouth that sang out the song of the girl with the jelly shoes he'd met on the beach.

Thinking about how I would play it back for Steph brought her into the call,

and this was really the purpose of all the little sabotages I tried to execute on the job—a way to bring my real life into this strange isolation I would go into and emerge from with cash. I held my girlfriend in my hands and I could hear her laughing, the snotty cackle that meant she was laughing at someone stupid.

Everyone loved the song. I played it for so many people I memorized the words, we both did, me and Steph, and we would sing it together and bust up laughing. Later, back in Boston, we called John the john mercilessly. I had stopped seeing him shortly before of the end of our vacation, when it got too real. John thought I was his girlfriend. I knew this was at least partly my fault, and it scared me. How was I able to do such a convincing job of pretending I really liked him? I didn't want to be such a good actress, a good liar, but there I was. What they call a natural.

John gave me the teal terry cloth robe, he picked a fat green bud from the film canister that held his pot and he tossed it on the counter beside me. For you and your boyfriend, he'd sneered jealously. Back at Brad's adobe, Steph stuffed the skunky cluster into her bong and greedily sucked it all up.

Thanks John, she singsonged, exhaling a giant puff of smoke.

Me and Steph sang all of John the john's folk songs onto his answering machine.

We mimicked his affected singing voice, howling, crooning. Visiting friends would join us, a chorus of mockery. I'm Playing Your Tape To Everyone, I gushed evil into the phone, I'm Playing Your Stupid Fucking Songs To Hundreds Of Aspiring Folk Singers. The last time we pulled this kind of shenanigan it really backfired. We'd crank called a weird, computer geek shut-in I'd had a call with. He had paused, mid-hump, to tell me about the time he worked for his college radio station and got to interview Lemmy. When he pulled out of me, the baggy condom was wet with pinkish-red blood. I had my period. Oh, My God! I emoted in my shrill hooker-voice. I Got It Early! Really I'd had it for a few days. The tampon I'd yanked out of my snatch in his bathroom was bundled in toilet paper and resting in my purse. Do I get a discount, he asked, snide, since you're bleeding? It's Actually Extra, I snapped. But I'll Let It Go. Since You Know Lemmy And Everything. Me, Steph and Dinah tortured this guy with a string of cruel and manic phone calls, but he used his advanced computer geek technology to call us back and leave the venomous tirade on our own answering machine. It was terrifying. Having barely ever touched a computer—this was the early 90s—I had no idea what information his little hacker gizmos were able find. Did he have our phone number now, our address, our names and social security numbers? Was he coming to vandalize our house or perhaps try to hurt us, was he siccing the cops on us or perhaps selling our identities to a an identity scam artist? For weeks the three of us rolled through the night, twitching with various nightmares, all of which seemed real in sleep and possible upon waking.

Whoring is lousy work.

I forgot to tell that to my friend Magdalena who called from New York to ask me how much she could expect to make, what she should wear and what about her tattoos. I forgot to tell her about how it makes you mean, makes you vengeful; how it turns you into a greedy monster because no matter how much money they are giving you it is never enough, and you start to want their blood, their homes, their self-esteem lying wet in the wastebucket like a shucked condom.

Dusted

Me and Steph separated. Steph went back to Tucson, to stay once more with Brad and Tulip; I remained behind in our salty, slanted Provincetown shanty. But only for so long. I felt like my life was on hold. The in-call, which I had not quit, felt hollower without her. What was I doing with my life? I called Steph from the pay phone in the parking lot across the street and she told me to come and be with her in the desert.

In my absence, there in Tucson, Steph had acquired a boyfriend. A guy named Rob. We'd met him at a party during our visit, standing amidst the woks full of stir-fry, the glasses of Mescal brought over the border, and a tub of sangria Steph had made herself, infusing jugs of cheap Carlo Rossi with cinnamon sticks and thick cuts of citrus. Of all people, Rob. Not even a hippie, not a part of any subculture, not even a laughable one. How could Rob measure up to Steph's strict, endless political criteria? He was a man, for starters. I couldn't really get past that to wonder if he was a vegetarian. He was dull. Brad's roommate Tulip had nicknamed him Dud, privately.

At the party Steph had set herself up with a bong and a pack of tarot cards, and set about divining the futures of the other guests.

Rob had crouched there on the floor, his long legs folded awkwardly, listening intently as Steph explained the round cards. She used a lesbian deck, that was why the cards were round. I thought that Steph shouldn't be giving men tarot readings with a lesbian deck. Hadn't she said that to me once? It was hard to remember which thoughts were originally mine, which were hers. Rob told her that he'd gotten his fortune told by a psychic once, and she had told him that he'd be a victim for the rest of his life. Now Steph that had hooked up with him I figured it was probably true.

I tried to have an open mind about Steph's new boyfriend Rob, but it really put a damper on our reunion

. I'd imagined some sweaty desert sex on a borrowed futon, but instead we were sitting awkwardly on the porch of Brad and Tulip's adobe; inside our hosts were cleaning up and trying not to eavesdrop.

Unlike Steph, I'd never had a problem with bisexuality. She was the one who'd claimed bisexual women were cowards, too chicken to live the lesbian life with gusto. I didn't bother pointing out her hypocrisy, I didn't want to seem petty. I understood the rule of the heart, it was: the heart ruled. Steph was not breaking up with me, she made this very clear. She wanted us both, me and Rob. I let it sink in. I had arrived in Tucson only an hour ago, two hours, everything was sinking in. I was a mess of pores, absorbing. Steph had so much stuff stuff to tell me. Like how she'd lied about being molested by a priest, also lied about being raped on the street. These two traumatic events were part of her identity, the key to understanding everything about her—her anger, her spontaneous violence, her impossibly high standards for the behavior of others. And they simply weren't true, had never happened.

That priest was probably a molester anyway, she spat. They all are.

And no one believed me anyway. She seemed bitter still that she hadn't been believed, even as she admitted her enormous lie. But there was a reason for such a grand manipulation. The reason she'd fabricated these tales of sexual assault, she explained, was because she'd actually been raped by her maternal grandfather throughout her entire life, from infancy to age eighteen. And every single assault had been forgotten, smooshed by her consciousness into some basement in her brain. She was remembering it all now for the first time, because he had died recently, a month or so ago. She'd read in books how that is very common among sexually abused women, to not remember any of the attacks until the perpetrator was dead. She looked at me intently, her eyes shining. I thought of all the stories I'd heard about her rape. How she'd fought horribly with her boyfriend at the time, she said he'd been so insensitive. How she had to take an extended leave of absence from her nannying job, and the mother had been so understanding, paying her anyway to help her through the trauma.

Dinah had told me how Steph showered fully clothed after it had happened,

how she had to be dragged from the shower and the soaking clothes peeled from her body.

How Dinah had supported Steph after it happened, I mean financially. How she'd saved her money to take them both to Jamaica, so Steph could be far from the wintry Boston street she'd been attacked on. All along I'd been acting out, because of my grandfather, Steph explained. Her face was full of pain and excitement. It hadn't occurred to her that this new information could be angering, could be confusing or scary to receive. On the contrary, it was a display of how deeply victimized Steph had been—so unfathomably scarred that she was forced to create these gargantuan lies, suckering all around her. It wasn't Steph that did this, it was her grandfather, via Steph's violated body. Steph had filed a police report about her false rape on a snowy Beacon Hill side street; when shown a bunch of mug shots she'd pinned a real face to her fiction. She went to court and testified against him, flanked by her mother and Dinah. The man went to jail. A lot of women were testifying against him, he'd really raped them, and I'm sure my testimony helped put him in prison, she said. She sounded proud. I sat silently. Rob is on his way over, she said. Right now. What? I asked. Numbness was eroding into fresh anxiety. He's bringing some beer, we can all hang out. Steph, I Am Not Hanging Out With Rob. I couldn't be that noble. There had to be some room in here for me. Maybe I had needs, too. It seemed that I should, that most people did, but I had a hard time locating mine. I didn't need much. I barely needed food, doubted I needed water at all. I could subsist on practically nothing, I was a cactus.

I did need a place to stay.

My scant belongings were packed into a gigantic, military-issue duffel bag. I had acquired a hand drum, I had that with me. too. A Middle Eastern drum, with a decorative silver body, and a plastic drum head that didn't sound nearly as good as the animal skin drum heads but I wasn't about to play drums on a dead animal. I had bought the drum in Provincetown right before I left, in a last ditch effort to make friends there. There was a women's drum circle once a week at the beach, and I thought if I had a drum I could go and be spiritual with a bunch of women and maybe be less lonely. I went once, the women were all a lot older than me, they looked at me with that yankee suspicion. No one spoke to me, and the tiny sound of my drum was obliterated by their enormous drums of tree trunk and hide. These women were serious, hand-drumming was their thing. Their drums were enormous, sculptured chunks of nature, they straddled the instruments like horses and began to pound, the heels of their boots digging into the wet, packed sand. On my long walk back to my room above Commercial Street I'd been picked up by an elderly couple who felt bad for me, walking down the long, long highway with my tiny drum, all alone. They drove me back to the center of town, and I'd thanked them. I hated the drum, but I'd spent a hundred dollars on it so felt compelled to bring it with me to Tucson. Now me and the drum would have to find a place to sleep. I'd assumed I'd be staying at Brad and Tulip's house, on the spare futon with Steph, but the homey adobe was now contaminated with the presence of the approaching Rob, strutting up the cacti-trimmed walkway, a six-pack of beer in his hand.

Tulip's friend was out of town, and Tulip had the keys so she could water the plants and feed the girl's cat. I went there, a ten-minute walk away. A hot, empty house with an ancient fan built into the adobe wall in the living room. It sent out a sigh of cool air. There was a bed, a sprawling messy futon scattered with torn foam egg crates and sheets. The girl was a hippie like Tulip, and her cupboard was stocked with tinctures and herbs. I made myself a stiff cup of valerian tea to deaden my emotions, and squirted a bunch of goldenseal beneath my tongue, wincing at the bitter medicine. All this stress was going to make me sick, I knew it would. I uncorked a bottle of wine I'd bought at the Circle K on the walk over, and got to work drinking it. Double-fisted, valerian and the grape. I sat down with my tarot deck, the same lesbian deck Steph used. The lovers card was a black woman and a white woman embracing before an enormous glowing vagina. There was an optional male card, a pagan Pan that looked Michael Jackson, skipping over a hill with some children. I didn't use it. If there was going to be a Pan I wanted him to look bawdy and wasted, mead spilled into his bard and a giant hard-on. A mischievous, faggoty Pan would also work, just not this sensitive new age babysitter. I was asking the tarot what I should do. I couldn't stay in Tucson, the smallest town in the world, with Steph and her new boyfriend. And I couldn't go back to Boston. I couldn't leave Boston and then come crawling back again, it was pathetic. I'd rather hike out into the desert and die. My friend Vinnie was in San Francisco, I thought about going there.

I flipped the cards over.

The front door opened and Steph walked into the house.

I hadn't locked the door, it was Tucson. She was sporting a tie-dyed shirt, rainbow-colored. A scarf around her head, some cords of golden hair dropping out in tangles. It was all Tulip's clothing. There had been a moment earlier, when Steph had sat me down and began with the ominous I have something to tell you, that I thought she was going to tell me she was in love with Tulip. She was decked out in all of Tulip's hippie accessories, and was appropriating our her loving yet edgy, laid-back vibe. What Are You Doing Here? I asked resentfully as she shut the door behind her. I gathered my cards up quickly, not wanting to give her a peek at my inner workings. I staggered them back into the pack, eyeing her warily, like a raccoon that had hopped through a window: cute, but possibly rabid. Usually I gave everything to Steph, hopped like a little frog as she entered a room, but I was liking the idea of being mad at her. At having a real reason to be. I was liking the idea of spending the night alone in this southwestern apartment, drinking wine, reading my cards again and again until I was drunk enough to fall asleep on the disheveled futon.

Come sit with me, Steph patted the couch beside her.

I climbed up from the floor and walked over with my bottle. I don't know what to do, she moaned breathlessly. I love you, and I feel really drawn to Rob. I'm so confused, and then there's everything with my grandfather, I'm really going through a lot. I don't want to loose you. I just sat there, silently, coldly. I slid the deep green neck of the bottle between my lips and drank. My wine glass sat on the floor by the tarot cards. How was your reading? she asked. What did the cards say? I shrugged. I wasn't going to help her decipher her own mysteries by probing mine. Michelle, why won't you walk to me? she whined. I shrugged again.

Steph twisted, frustrated. Then she tensed, and flung herself onto my lap, her head pressed into my belly, her arms wound around me tightly.

Oh my god I'm having a body memory!

she yelped. She convulsed across my thighs for a minute, waiting for my hands to descend upon her in gentle caresses. I gripped the wine bottle, dug into the gluey label with my thumbnail. She sat back up again, and shook out her shoulders. Oh my god, I could just . . . feel my grandfather's penis inside me. Has that ever happened to you? I felt sick. I mean, a body memory. Have you ever had one? I shook my head. I didn't believe Steph, not at all. Despite the dull heaviness of the wine, that purple blanket, and the cups of valerian tea, I felt lucid. I looked clearly at Steph. Michelle, what? her voice was rising with a desperate tinge. Steph was a sociopath. She was psychotic, she was a liar, a dangerous, dangerous liar. You Have To Leave, I told her, standing up. The floor wavered a bit beneath me, I was drunk. Maybe drunk enough to sleep. What? she cried. I Can't Help You Figure This Out, You Have To Go. But I need you! she cried. I mean, she didn't actually cry—in fact, I realized then, Steph never cried. I had never seen her shed a tear, not once, not over anything. Not when Brad was diagnosed positive, not while retelling the tales of her many abuses, not when we fought, or broke up, or reunited. Not when she fought with her family via telephone. Never. Rob doesn't understand how hard this is, she continued, having these memories about my grandfather. YOU understand. He doesn't. I figured she'd make him understand soon enough. I figured that Rob the Dud, the eternal victim, would soon be paying dearly for all that Steph had survived, real and imagined.

For about a week I lived a strange life inside a stranger's house. I didn't know where the original occupant had gone, or when she would be back, but Tulip seemed unconcerned about it on her daily visits to make sure the plants were watered, the cats fed, and that I was still alive. I left the house once a day, when the intense heat and sunlight woke me up in the early morning. I would walk down the street to the health food store and buy orange juice for breakfast, and a trusty container of hummus for lunch, if I could stand to eat. I bought bundles of valerian to replace all I'd used, and then more to keep using. The walk back would be difficult already with the increasing, unbelievable heat. I'd feel lightheaded, and pause for a moment in some found shade, then trudge on. Back at my borrowed home I would drink the juice, boil water for the valerian root, and start a cold bath. I'd take a towel out into the scrubby backyard, and lay beneath the scorching sun for about ten minutes. Then I'd pull myself up, wobble back into the house with spots forming in my vision, and collapse into the icy tub. I felt like if I kept doing this I'd have a mystical experience, but the valerian tea subdued my energy, and I retreated to the futon with a book, Leslie Marmon Silko, and my tarot deck.

I picked card upon card until my future was an indecipherable blend of fire and water, earth and air.

Tulip would visit and sink down into the futon with me, wrap herself around me.

She was a very touchy person. She'd play with my hair and I was grateful for the contact. I felt like a child in a sickbed, and I didn't know what I'd do if Tulip stopped her daily visits. We picked cards, and gossiped. She thought Steph was crazy, which reassured me. I didn't tell her that I thought Steph was lying about her grandfather. It was too taboo, doubting a girl's abuse. I didn't want Tulip to think I was bad, what if she stopped coming by. I had decided that Steph would stay with Rob and that they'd have babies. Steph wanted a baby badly, she'd talked about it all the time but I'd thought it was only another of her big dreams, like robbing banks and blowing up movie theaters. Will Steph get pregnant? Tulip asked the tarot, and drew the lover's card. Wow, She's Really Going To Have Babies With Rob, I said. It was seeping in, the deep reality of my predicament. This was it. No more Steph, not ever again, and here I was in Arizona staving off the panic attack of my life with bundles of this smelly root that stunk like feet. Steph was shocked and horrified when she learned that the tarot forecast her destiny as mother of Rob the Dud's babies. No, I won't! I'm Not getting pregnant! she yelled. Don't pick cards about me when I'm not there! But it was all we did. Tulip seemed to be enjoying the drama. Not in a mean way. Tucson's such a dull town is all, not much happens. Is Steph Insane? I asked the deck, and it gave me a card symbolizing mental anguish. Yup.

I decided I would leave. I would go to San Francisco, and stay with Vinnie. I wondered what San Francisco would be like. I realized there would be girls, lots and lots of girls. Probably I'd find one I'd like, and fall in love. Lots and lots of lesbian girls. The jittery panic made its holy transformation into a sort of adrenaline that gushed through my body. I thought about the little book that I'd been writing poems in. In San Francisco I would be with girls and I would write poetry. I would write lots and lots of poetry and be with lots and lots of girls and I'd be happy. I had a plan. I was awash with gratitude at having a plan, I was filled with relief, felt suddenly capable. I'd never had a plan before, not one of my own. I told it to Tulip on her next visit. I'd been on the phone all morning, reserving plane tickets, booking a shuttle to the Phoenix airport. Tulip was surprised. Wow, she said. I think she was sad to have me go. She was a nurturing type, maternal, and with me gone it was back to Brad, her large brood of cats, and Steph's neurosis. Really? she asked, suspicious. Aren't you sad? You're going to leave Steph? Briefly I worried about my lack of sadness. Was I just repressing something, pushing it all into my mind's secret chambers like a traumatized girl? I shook my head. No, No, I said, I Can't Wait, I Have To Go! Filled with new purpose. It had to be important, such an intense and spontaneous change. It had to be filled with meaning. I was going into my destiny. It's My Destiny, I said to Tulip, who nodded, quite serious. She was a hippie, and understood spiritual things. It was the vocation I'd waited so patiently for in Catholic school, concentrating inside a church, listening for the voice of god to tell me what I should do with my life.

I was being called to San Francisco.

The shuttle to Phoenix picked me up at Brad and Tulip's adobe, where I sat squirming. Steph pouted. What will you do? she asked. Write, I said. I'm Going To Be A Writer. And Hang Out With Lesbians. Steph was eating a little noodle salad from the health food store, I kept grabbing the plastic fork from her hand and eating it. Hey! She tried to grab it back. You're eating all of it! You Have Ruined My Appetite For Days, I said. You Should Be Buying Me Dinner. Tulip laughed. Up the dusty southwestern street the shuttle bus cruised. Tulip crushed me in a very sincere hug. I didn't really want to touch Steph, who looked weighted to her seat with the many bong hits she'd done that morning. I squeezed her shoulder. Have A Good Time With Rob, I said, and she scowled. I Mean It, I said. Have A Nice Life. Here, In Tucson. With Rob. I wasn't trying to make fun of her, but it sounded so pathetic. Tucson and Rob.

I left her there in the dust.

Tattoo You

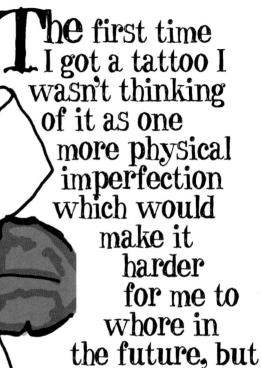

The first time I got a tattoo I wasn't thinking of it as one more physical imperfection which would make it harder for me to whore in the future, but it was.

I already had some strikes against me, but they were slight and easily remedied. In general, the fact that I was female and in possession of a vagina trumped any of my less appealing attributes. The guys aren't picky. Maybe they won't return to you in the future, but chances are, once they're in the room with you they're not leaving. Though there was that one call who turned and walked back to the elevator after I answered the door in my black skintight tank dress, wiry bits of armpit hair curling out from beneath my arms. Later, he called. He said, I was at your place once before and the girl I saw, she, she wasn't right. His voice actually held a note of real fear. It was me—Bev—on the telephone. I thought about my coworkers at the in-call. What terrible secrets were they hiding beneath their merry widows? What uncouth behavior emerged behind the closed bedroom door? Did someone have a tumor? Speak in tongues, have a trigger-happy gag reflex?

I pressed the frightened caller for details. She just wasn't right, he insisted. He sounded like he was from Southie. He sounded like a working-class punk. The deeper into Boston's pits you go, the thicker the accent. Maybe You Got The Wrong Place, I said. My own rough New England accent was emerging from whatever neuro-linguistic region it had been banished to a million years ago. It creeped back under certain circumstances—fury, extreme inebriation, conversation with people whose similar accents bulged and flexed like a muscle in their mouths. None Of Our Girls Are Weird, I insisted. Pronounced 'weird' 'weeeeid.' Heavy on the vowel, hold the 'r'. Maybe Bev was from Southie, too, I thought. Beverly Riordan, hardworking Irish girl. No, it was your place, the traumatized trick kept yapping. Comm Ave, near Blanchards? Call from the pay phone at the CVS? Yeah, I relented, That Sounds Like Our House. The girl, he said, beginning to crack. She had hair where she's not supposed to. In her armpit. He sounded a little angry, like he'd been duped into nearly fucking a bona fide carnival freak, a snake-skinned woman, her cheeks thick with fur, hands that morphed into fleshy pincers. That Was ME! I hooted into the phone. I Don't Shave My Armpits. My laughter crackled into the receiver and burst staticy into my own ear. It's Wicked French, Dude! Fuck you, he spat, and hung up.

Guys hate being laughed at. Especially by prostitutes.

So the marks against my marketability as a prostitute, besides my hairy armpits, were my hairy legs and, depending on personal preference, my hairy snatch. My small breasts, cleaved to my ribs with lack of meat, dairy, or any nutrition whatsoever—they were a plus or minus. Same with my too-skinny physique. My hair also rode the line. At its best it was a short, black 'do I could shape into a feminine wispiness with gel, an elfin cap, a modern flapper. At its worst it was unsalvageable, stiff from bleaching. The texture of dry grass with the color of healthy grass, a short, spiky, brilliant green hairdo with no discernible shape, just growing in from a season of requisite lesbian baldness. But a wig could be dropped on that disaster—long, synthetic auburn locks that bobbed in thick rolls, or the classic black Cleopatra-style wig, always the cheapest wig at any wig shop, every sex worker had one. Everything about me that couldn't fit the dominant beauty standard could be glossed over or hidden, except tattoos. The men wouldn't care—in the brutal words of Steph, They just want a wet hole. But management, conservative in this industry as management anywhere, didn't like hiring tattooed girls. Every whorehouse owner-operator liked to imagine theirs the cream of the crop, a real high-class enterprise, the exception to the sleaze stereotype. Having tattooed girls made a house seem low-rent. Especially tattoos that couldn't be stashed under a swath of cloth. A butterfly on the ass would escape the critical gaze of the boss and then it's just between you and the john, who no doubt could give a shit.

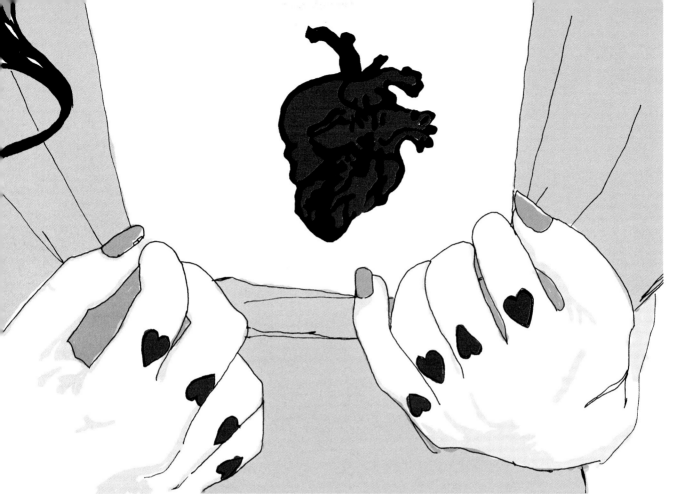

But my first tattoo wasn't pretty.

It was a gory, blood-red anatomical heart floating on the skin above my actual heart, unmoored by artery and vein. It was hard to hide from my boss at the San Francisco in-call where I briefly worked, but I figured it out. The high rise of my dress or blouse left me at a disadvantage during line-up, where I looked comparatively bulky and prudish amidst the strappy halters, the dresses that sashed 'round necks and dove toward delicate bellybuttons. Even a simple v-neck revealed the smeary red and black aorta. Beside the basic inappropriateness of a female having a tattoo at all, let alone one lifted from a medical textbook and stuck half onto her boob, there was also the part of it not being a very good tattoo, artistically speaking. If I told you I'd gotten it poked onto me in prison you would perhaps believe me. Again, there is a john for every sort of hooker, and there no doubt lived one who would enjoy a joyless hour with a starving vegan with a grisly anatomical heart smeared across her tiny breast, but management would never go for it.

When I quit whoring in Boston and then later returned to it in San Francisco, I had forgotten how much I hated it. It wasn't like the kind of hate I felt for other shitty jobs, though people like to say things like 'all work is prostitution'. Most work is exploitation, but most work is not prostitution. Prostitution is prostitution, a very specific sort of exploitation wholly unlike my other miserable jobs scooping hummus at the cafe, ringing up beef jerky at the corner store, scheduling perms at the hair salon, mindlessly xeroxing business papers at the copy shop. And, while I am doling out literal corrections to flippant turns of phrase, the earth doesn't get raped. It gets mined and poisoned and blown up and depleted, it gets ruined, but it doesn't get raped. Alright, then.

While I have always resented every job I have ever had—

even, truth be told, the rather glamorous job of sitting here in my kitchen drinking black coffee and scribbling my self-obsessed musings into my notebook, easily the greatest job I have ever had, better then I ever hoped for—while I have always resented my job, no labor has ever felt excruciating in the way prostitution did. And once I did it I knew that I could always do it, survive it, and it is lodged now forever in my most desperate places, a final fall-back plan. It's like alcoholism, that same sort of lure. So heady at first, a rush, a high and I couldn't quite believe I was actually doing it. I was detached from myself, sort of split and watching it like a great movie: my life.

And holy fuck the money—
one hundred dollar bills.

I'd never held one before, crinkling in my hand. But it was a downward progression, a steady depression, letting people I didn't like have full access to my body. Letting people who didn't like me fuck me. It wore me out. So I stopped, but the hooks are lodged in my greedy, fearful mouth. Wanting so much and afraid I'll never get it. I mean money of course, and the placid mind you hope it can purchase. I'd be busting my ass, get a check for a hundred and fifty dollars at the end of the week and I'd think—how could I help it: I could've made that in an hour. Maybe hooking wasn't so bad. I could deal with it better cause I'm older now, I'm smarter, less damaged and not vegan—I can cope better. And my brain keeps clicking—an hour? Shit, I could've made that week's pay in forty-five minutes. And I'd have a story. I'd have that sex-worker-chic outlaw shine. What do I have now, dispatching delivery cars in a cold office that won't let me have rips in my clothing and all my clothing is torn? What do I have now, raising money on the telephone to save trees and woodland creatures, getting it on a credit card, hustling to make a quota, sweet-talk and guilt in equal measure. So many ways to beg. And I would forget how much I hate whoring the way an alcoholic forgets how much she hates to get drunk. Go back and try it again, different this time.

Every time I get a tattoo I think, Oh you can't whore with that.

They won't hire you. Dense spaceships along my arm, a grey-black ink that bleeds at the edges, fuzzy. The hazy blue sky around them, the stretched-out yellow stars they dart around. A crazed looking little girl on my other arm, a devil on a Big Wheel with ponytails and a Band-Aid. People always ask Oh, that's you, isn't it? and I say No, cause it's not. How awful, to get your own self tattooed onto yourself. I mean, I'm bad but I'm not that bad.

The big red roses that healed so poorly because I kept snorting speed and not sleeping and banging it around. They're sort of feminine, the roses, edged in yellow and pink, but they're also sort of biker-lady, and the way the green leaves fan out onto my hand well you know what hand tattoos get called. No Future tattoos. Like fingers, necks and faces.

Like the little hearts that glow crimson from my knuckles.

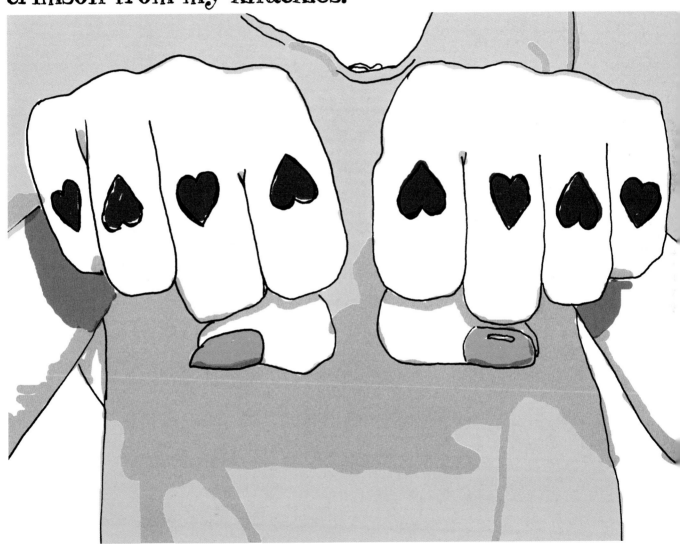

The skull and crossbones, the nautical star, the ones I got poked into my skin by a friend, with a needle wrapped in thread and a bottle of india ink. The firecracker on my back shoulder that actually looks like a tampon.

So many words, script that curls into itself or letters fashioned with serifs and loops.

Doubt, Excess, Kills. A dagger on the back of my calf reads Pure tragedy, the blueish length of it pointing down to a jailhouse pinprick poison-bottle, marked XXX and leaking bubbles that pop, cartoon-style.

A fucking pigeon on the back of my shoulder, crowned, King of the Street. An angry-looking mermaid on my stomach, her shoulders broad, her tits hard like pecs, her ass shaded red like the glow on her sunburned cheeks. Her legs blur into a fishtail. My love's initial stabbed into a heart on my forearm. a viney flower near my thumb, so faint it looks like a fake one half-washed from my skin. For a while every tattoo was a reminder that I didn't want my body to be saleable. Each one worked to make me unhireable should I forget my resolve and, tempted by cash and laziness, tried again.

That's how it was for a little while,
until they simply became my body.

Pluto Drive —
San Francisco, 2000

I was going through a Pluto transit.

I tell you this, like I tell you everything, not to excuse my behavior but to explain it. Pluto, the planet that rules death and destruction and also transformation, transformation and shit. By shit I am not being casual. Pluto rules excrement, it rules surgery, it rules blood and pus and everything exploding. Imploding, too.

With a Pluto transit you are left open, vulnerable, to certain influences. Things begin to fascinate you. Pluto rules obsession, its very nature. All that is beneath is ruled by Pluto. The id floats to the surface, gently. You're not even aware there's been a regime change. Who 's calling the shots now? Your psyche. I began to buy taxidermy. Or rather I began to want to buy taxidermy. I had possessive feelings toward the frozen growls, the plastic teeth bared, the glass eyes that rolled with light. The furred face stretched over a base of styrofoam. Have you ever seen the raw materials of a taxidermist? It's almost creepier then the dead animal that gets slapped around it. I was traveling a lot, across America, and the country is filled with dead animals. In Las Vegas you can buy fake jackalopes mounted on tiny plaques. Jackalopes of course do not exist, they're taxidermied rabbit heads, the small face frozen in a nervous flinch, startled, with the antlers of some kind of deer jammed onto its head. You could buy one for sixty dollars, at The World's Largest Gift Shop, and when I won the bingo jackpot over at the Showboat I almost bought one. I won like a thousand dollars but I didn't buy the jackalope. Sixty dollars just seemed too much. In a barn in upstate New York I saw tons of taxidermy. Mostly birds, grouse and turkey and quail. Dust on the feathers. The taxidermy in Montana was tremendous and had won awards. I'm serious. Top prizes. A mountain lion, the broken neck of a deer twisted in its plastic teeth. The eyes of the deer gleamed, enormous with fright and pain. It looked like something you would find in a church, it was breathtaking. These things cost thousands of dollars if they're for sale at all. I could only afford an alligator head. Small and hard, the teeth real, yellowy and sharp. They sell them by the bucket in New Orleans. Their hollow jaws. Besides my Plutonian attraction to the alligator head and its marble eyes, there was nostalgia. My grandparents had had one in their kitchen when I was little, and it was such a curiosity—the fanged, decapitated head of a southern swamp animal sitting on a little shelf in a New England kitchen. It sat among other knickknacks, mostly souvenirs from summer road trips: plastic Amish dolls, a boy and a girl; a small ceramic Mexican man sleeping under his sombrero from South of the Border in the Carolinas; lots of snow globes. Papa's alligator head was the spooky and ferocious centerpiece. It was fascinating. Who knew they sold such things, in the lands beyond Massachusetts? I had never even seen a live one.

The alligator heads are shellacked, they look plastic. It's hard to imagine they were ever alive.

I have a giant paperweight with the amber body of a scorpion encased in its thick domed center. I have a few of these—one with a skinny black widow spider, one of its eight legs snapped off in the epoxy, an air bubble suspended beside it, capturing the motion. A tarantula, its thick and hairy legs. The head of a rattlesnake, it's mouth gaped open. You can buy the entire taxidermied snake at roadside outfits throughout the southwest, their bottoms curled, the length of them springing up, these carefully shaped dead snakes, fangs bared, they're expensive. I have a fetal shark in a jar of formaldehyde. The formaldehyde is tinted with food coloring the sharp blue of swimming pools, and a sticker on the styrofoam base reads shark. The shark's eyes are wide and dark, its body small, tail curled up. The Florida souvenir shop where I bought it, a tented warehouse that stunk of beach rot and blared Rush Limbaugh also sold a squid-in-formaldehyde series, but they cost more and lacked the blue tint job. The place sold puffer fish and the razored brown skeletons of horseshoe crabs, but I wasn't attracted to these things. They smelled sour and lacked the strange romance of say, the hide of a rabbit, the fur dyed hot fuchsia.

So my Pluto transit had rendered me soft to the allure of dead animals, self-destructive teenagers, and drugs.

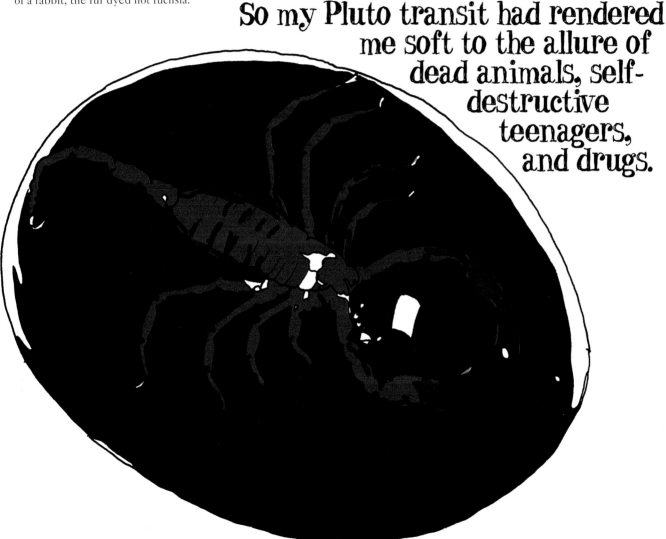

Eleanor was eighteen. In the past I had mostly rolled my eyes when people my own age dramatically obsessed over the teenaged or the recently-teen. It was just like when dykes obsessed over straight girls, the pull of whatever you can't have stoking the fires of a deep self-loathing. I mean, it looked dumb from the outside—too revealing of your psychological state, not romantic, pathological and played. But I fell in love with Eleanor quickly. She wasn't a drug addict, but she had been. She was so young, to have had a drug addiction in her past meant, what, that she'd been snorting meth when she was fifteen years old? Exactly. My little after school special. I liked how dirty and fucked up it felt to be with someone so young, and Eleanor liked how dirty and fucked up it felt to be with someone verging on thirty, and, both of us imagining ourselves beyond corruption personally, set about trying to corrupt the other. Swiftly Eleanor moved into my house. She went from the girl I had met on a road trip to the girl living in my bedroom. Which my roommates must have loved. Having lived there the longest, in a Mission district house that was little more then a glorified squat where anarchy reigned, I felt that I could do whatever I wanted. Which had included, previously, harboring a runaway from Washington state with really poor hygiene and social skills, and, presently, allowing a couple of middle-class young lesbians to crash in the loft in the back room while leisurely looking for both housing and jobs, and shuffling Eleanor into my bedroom, never to leave again. She didn't pay rent. I wanted to retain the right to kick her out at a moment's notice should our love sour, so I didn't take her money. Plus she had no money.

She was eighteen years old.

Eleanor walked into the bookstore where I worked.

I loved to look up from the register and see her, hesitant at the edge of the counter, her sharp, dark face hovering above the Worst-Case Scenario book and the Bad Girls Guides and the other gifty impulse buys that littered the area. Her brown eyes throbbed their steady, hypnotic throb. We would go on my break together.

It was winter, and we had been girlfriends or whatever you might call it since the summer, but not consistently. It had been choppy. First I'd had to break up with the girl I'd been involved with at the time of the fateful road trip. Then I had to run off to New England for a few months, to freak out and decompress from the drama and drink heavily. Now, back in San Francisco, I was ready to commit to Eleanor. We thought perhaps we had been together in past lives. I had been her mother, or she had been my father. Maybe we'd been brother and sister, some sort of familial relationship that charged our frenzied fucking with taboos violated just beyond the bounds of our recognition. We would go into the restaurant beside my bookstore and order chocolate deep fried in won tons. The greasy package sizzled in our mouths, burst open, poured molten sweet down our throats. In the unisex bathroom we'd bolt the door and fuck, my leg stretched onto the sink, my breath fogging the mirror. I'd pull back from the wall and we'd gaze at our reflections. we couldn't believe ourselves, how hot we were. Our mutual attraction made us both better looking, my tits grew in her palms

We wanted to go to Greece.

Eleanor's family was partly from Hawaii and partly from Greece. The Grecian portion of the family was partly from Cyprus and partly from some village on, what, the mainland? Do they call it the mainland? The big island of Greece? Our sex, our obsessive passion, the thick Pluto influence, it was too rarefied and heavy for San Francisco. San Francisco felt somehow insubstantial, newfangled and cheap, soggy and mundane. The wet and grimy streets, the tired bars with their yeasty odors and bloating clientele. Our love was too precious for America, we needed Europe. We could go to my ancestral lands, but Poland seemed unromantic, or romantic in the wrong way, too cold and sausagey. Ireland made me think of all the asshole Irish people back in Massachusetts, we seemed doomed to die from a gay bashing in Ireland. My ethnic homelands were out, it had to be Greece, the birthplace of homosexuality, a place that understood poetry and longing and ancient lusts.

How would we get there?

Eleanor didn't really have a job. She hadn't yet needed one, as her expenses were small enough to be cared for with the profits of her vague pot-selling business. Her father in his suburban home grew pot in a narrow yard alongside their stucco home, tall green stalks with the famous leaves splayed like skinny green hands, shaking in the balmy California breeze. The suburbs were always warm and sunny. It didn't seem so bad, living out there, except girls seemed to get kidnapped at an alarming rate. Eleanor sold her dad's pot but she would have to steal it, from the yard or from his room, and he would catch her and they'd have screaming fights about what a loser Eleanor was and why didn't she go to college like her sister who was presently studying Russian literature at a respected private college in Oregon. Eleanor would relate the fight to me, fuming. I'd be like, Of Course Your Dad Is Pissed, Who AantsTheir Daughter To Be A Drug Dealer, but then I couldn't even wrap my head around a dad growing marijuana in his backyard in the first place, so I said nothing at all. Clearly the rules of the nuclear family were different out here in California, at the end of the twentieth century. I felt unequipped to make a statement so I just nodded my head in sympathy, losing myself in Eleanor's large and tilting eyes. Eleanor couldn't steal enough weed from her dad to turn the sort of profit that could send us to Greece. It wasn't like he was farming the stuff, it was just a small plot, a private garden, medicinal for his chronic migraines. I myself was making shit at the bookstore. I was making more then anyone else excepting the manager and I was making poop, eight-fifty and hour, and I was grateful for this, grateful and sheepish to be making a full dollar more then the rest of the workers. I figured I couldn't expect to make more then eight-fifty in any job, because I hadn't gone to college and I had tattoos on my fingers. Eight-fifty was king. We would never get to Greece.

We Should Sell Drug-Drugs, I said to Eleanor.

It was night and we were on my futon. I waved the origami bundle of cocaine we were about to enjoy, illustrating what I meant by Drug-Drugs. Real drugs, not leaves. I undid the cryptic angles of folded magazine paper to reveal a thin layer of flaky whiteness. It was bad cocaine. How bad exactly was anyone's guess; I'd probably never done truly good cocaine so my judgment was useless. At least it wasn't yellow like the tiny, cellophane knots of stuff you could get from the dealers who stood on the corner of Sixteenth and Mission.

This stuff had come from the Albino, affectionately called
the All-Wino,

**the only authentically
lousy bar remaining
in San Francisco.**

A big guy with a mullet and a leather vest hung out at the end of the bar, selling coke. Sometimes you'd slip him a twenty, easily procured from the handy ATM machine by the door or pieced together bill by bill, ones and five's, between you and two or three others, whoever had some extra cash to kick down for a line. You'd slip the man with the mullet twenty dollars and he would reach into his leather vest and palm you the tightly folded bindle.

Sometimes he would go with you into the women's bathroom, a cramped red place stuffed with cigarette smoke, the floor tiles broken and grimy and wet, a busted-up armchair in the corner. It was not uncommon to find a female lumped in the chair, wasted and crying.

It was that kind of place.

A single bathroom stall with a disturbingly low-cut door on a rickety hinge. It always felt like the entire bathroom could see you taking a piss, or balancing on the skanky bowl which too often overflowed, squeezing out a frantic cocaine shit. There was graffiti on the walls in the tight stall. Ice Cream Girl, a stick-figured girl with a triangular body and a ponytailed, crowned head, holding ice cream, another triangle topped with a circle. Grace, in loopy, dripping paint pen script. Cocaine Whores Your Death Is My Money. That one was creepy. That one was really fucked-up. I would stare at it as I wiped my ass, it was right there in magic marker, black scrawl on the red wall, eye-level. Glad I wasn't a money-giving death-having cocaine whore. Not like that one woman, Loo was her name, she looked so out of place at the

Albino, straight in the classic sense, not just heterosexual but square also, Financial District. She looked like an office worker—blunt, heavy hair, regular clothes. Always alone, always bumming a line in the bathroom where the drugs got busted out after the dealer left. I was trying to tell you how he's pull out a paper bag full of powder and just dip the square of paper into it, eye it, fold the package up quick with nimble fingers. Loo said, This is my last party, I'm going to rehab. I'm going to try sober living. Good Luck, I said sincerely. It sounded awful. The back of my throat was numb from the coke. Sometimes it made it hard to smoke, made me gag when the stream of hot cloud struck the numbness. I'd choke out a gust and my eyes would tear and I'd feel gross. Embarrassed. Pull the straw of my gin and tonic into my mouth and suck hard, the carbonation exploding onto the back of my throat, wake up.

I loved to smoke on coke.

And drink. And, I loved to smoke while I drank. And do lines. I would be sitting at my little table loving it all, keeping my smoke low, under the table because the anal bartender was working who would make you take your cigarette outside, and I would see Eleanor looking at me.

She would be at the jukebox,

which you had to play because if you didn't the bartenders would play their music and that was really bad, that was rap-rock CDs, that was Kid Rock and Limp Bizkit, so you had to keep on feeding dollars to the machine. Nights at the Albino could be pricey, but my rent was cheap, two hundred dollars. No bills because I hadn't stupidly gone to college, thank god. All extra money went to drinking and smoking and, with the recent discovery of the Albino and its resident dealer, now cocaine. You could ask people for money at the Albino, if you needed it. It was sort of family-ish. A dollar for a beer? Got a cigarette? Can I have a bump? It was communal. Everyone got real wasted, it was that kind of place. People would give you dollars and wonder the next morning where their money went. People would wake up the next day and try to remember everything. At the jukebox Eleanor played Nick Cave, Stagger Lee. So inky and evil, his voice sleazing sinister across the bar's moldy carpet. There were roaches at the Albino. Sometimes people came into the bathrooms to smoke crack, the acrid smoke would seep out and alert the bartenders who would kick them out. You had to draw the line somewhere. No crack allowed. I got my wallet stolen once. It was my own fault, leaving my army bag slung on the back of my chair, unsnapped. Dude slipped his hand in, grabbed my Virgin of Guadalupe wallet and split. I didn't even realize it until the next morning. I must've been getting my drinks for free that night.

Stagger Lee on the jukebox and Eleanor and I would go into the bathroom stall

that was the absolute worst to fuck in, with that door cut so low, a saloon door. The heel of my boot would be crashed down on the back of the toilet or else Eleanor would be sitting there, her feet on the toilet seat and me bent over, legs spread, bracing myself on the mottled red wall, Coke Whores Your Death My Money. Inevitably a team of females would come in, voices ringing, slurred. Who's in there? You're dykes, that's cool. Don't stop cause we're here ha ha ha.

Eleanor should sell coke.

 I was scraping the residual powder from the magazine page's deep creases, trying to knock a line onto the Marilyn Manson CD on the trunk at the foot of my futon. The trunk's surface was filled with clutter. Water glasses and forty ouncers of beer, half-empty Odwalla cartons and coffee cups. I mostly ingested liquids. Books, papers, a seashell grubby with cigarette ash and crushed butts. A couple pills, Xanax, also stolen from Eleanor's stressed-out father. Cellophane scraps and a razor blade that looked like it could be bearing tetanus. Where could we find cocaine to sell? Where were the cocaine wholesalers? All of our friends did the stuff, there was no shortage of customers. When did that happen? I remembered when no one did coke, and then when people chased it down for special occasions like new years or a birthday. Now it was, it's Wednesday night, let's do lines. It would be nice, I thought, to never again need to do the run-around, asking who had drugs. To never again need to be nice to someone you didn't like to get them, endure the up-down sweep of the mulleted dealer's gaze over your body as he scooped your parcel. To never again need to compete wit your jonesing friends to be the jonesing friend that your holding friend invited into the bathroom with her. The terrain of drug-scoring suddenly seemed dramatic and exhausting. Perhaps we were too involved? But in Greece we wouldn't be. We'd only have to plunge a little deeper into it in order to be gloriously free of it all. Yeah, said Eleanor. We had a little cash, her from her pot sales, me from doing some tarot readings at the lesbian bar. This was an investment. It would send us to Greece.

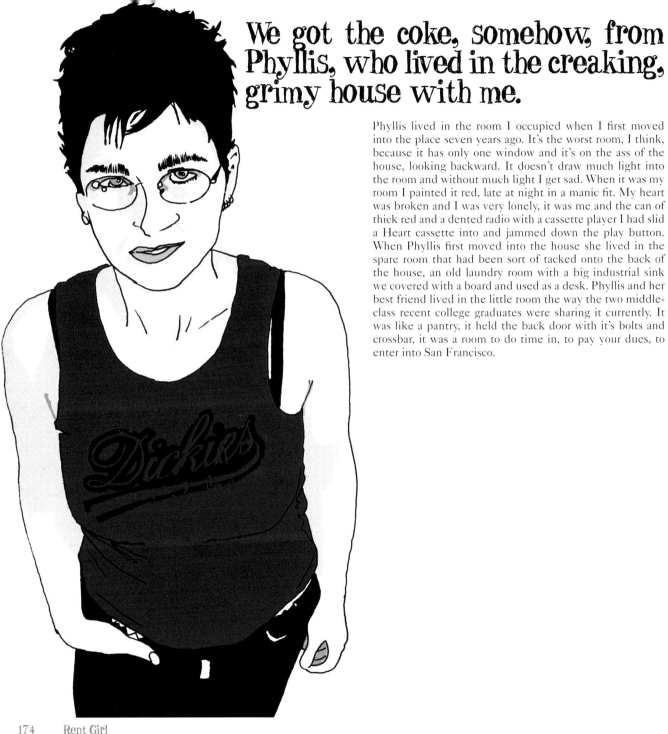

We got the coke, somehow, from Phyllis, who lived in the creaking, grimy house with me.

Phyllis lived in the room I occupied when I first moved into the place seven years ago. It's the worst room, I think, because it has only one window and it's on the ass of the house, looking backward. It doesn't draw much light into the room and without much light I get sad. When it was my room I painted it red, late at night in a manic fit. My heart was broken and I was very lonely, it was me and the can of thick red and a dented radio with a cassette player I had slid a Heart cassette into and jammed down the play button. When Phyllis first moved into the house she lived in the spare room that had been sort of tacked onto the back of the house, an old laundry room with a big industrial sink we covered with a board and used as a desk. Phyllis and her best friend lived in the little room the way the two middle-class recent college graduates were sharing it currently. It was like a pantry, it held the back door with it's bolts and crossbar, it was a room to do time in, to pay your dues, to enter into San Francisco.

The flat had another bedroom which belonged to my best friend Freddie who had sort of freaked out and taken off to Czechoslovakia. She was working a vague computer job over there, learning to speak Czech and drinking a lot of beer. She kept trying to get me to sell her shitty possessions because she was so low on money—her toaster oven, her espresso machine with the crust of petrified soy milk coating the milk steamer—but I couldn't get my head around it. Sell it where? To who? Would I have to clean it? Everything in the house was broken and dirty. If it wasn't when it was hauled into the place it would be shortly. Freddie's room was being sublet by Phyllis' girlfriend Marcia, who was too good for the place. She deserved better, was there out of pure desperation. Each day she would come home from her temp job, snap on some rubber gloves and resentfully wash our dishes. She would make them slam and clatter as she scrubbed, communicating her deep unhappiness with the situation. Marcia had put up curtains in Freddie's room, she had hung framed things on the walls.

Every day she cleaned the kitchen and every day the rest of us ruined it, leaving the mess to sit and connect with the rest of the mess.

The house was a giant, sprawling mess.

There was a jumble of straight-up trash at the top of the stairs, in the hall. It was the first thing you saw when you entered our flat, it greeted you. According to the principles of feng-shui, it's where an altar should be. We had a dark, magnificent heap of garbage. We had let it accumulate until there was more then the sanitation workers would collect. We had to bring it to the dump, but how? It sat there, growing, as we tried to solve its problem.

Phyllis got the cocaine and I guess what happened was first she took a bit for herself,

part of the deal for having found us a wholesaler. Marcia did some as well, and then they had a three-way with Ramona, that very night, at my house. They all laid around on Phyllis' unmade bed, in her room that smelled like mouse because of the mouse that lived in a cage on Phyllis' bookshelf. It peed and scratched in wood chips which were rarely changed. Phyllis and Marcia and Ramona fucked and snorted my coke and then brought the rest of it over to Under a Rock where, for some strange reason, I was.

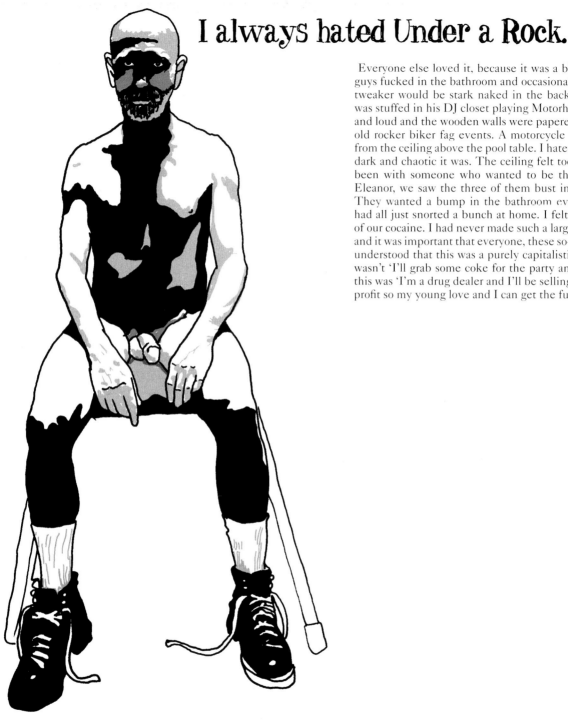

I always hated Under a Rock.

Everyone else loved it, because it was a biker fag bar and guys fucked in the bathroom and occasionally some elderly tweaker would be stark naked in the back, where the DJ was stuffed in his DJ closet playing Motorhead. It was dark and loud and the wooden walls were papered with flyers for old rocker biker fag events. A motorcycle hung by chains from the ceiling above the pool table. I hated how small and dark and chaotic it was. The ceiling felt too low. I must've been with someone who wanted to be there. I was with Eleanor, we saw the three of them bust in with our coke. They wanted a bump in the bathroom even though they had all just snorted a bunch at home. I felt very protective of our cocaine. I had never made such a large drug purchase and it was important that everyone, these so-called 'friends', understood that this was a purely capitalistic venture. This wasn't 'I'll grab some coke for the party and we'll split it', this was 'I'm a drug dealer and I'll be selling this to you at a profit so my young love and I can get the fuck to Greece.'

Well, can I buy a bag, then?

Ramona was asking. Ramona was used to simply charming her drugs off of people. Plus she always generously shared her portions with me, so I felt a twinge of badness at this new dynamic—me having bunches of drugs, withholding it from the famously poor Ramona, making her pony up twenty dollars for a taste. The cold world of capitalism. I Have To Bag It Up, I hollered at her over the Metallica. We would have to drive out to the suburbs where Eleanor's drug-selling paraphernalia was. And we did, right then. It was midnight. We could be back to Under A Rock by one, sell two or three bags before the bar closed. I left the bar with a mostly full gin and tonic tucked under my coat, drank it in Eleanor's Jetta as we zoomed down the freeway. The night felt dark and creepy, I hated that bar. It had bad vibes, and they had infected me. I sucked at the dregs of my cocktail and stuffed the tainted glass under my seat. Can I Smoke? I asked Eleanor. If I Smoke Out The Window? Eleanor shrugged, which meant no, but if she couldn't advocate for herself what was I supposed to do? A shrug meant I'd Rather You Didn't, but I liked directness. I couldn't be a mind-reader. I pulled a Camel out of the pack in my purse, rolled down the window.

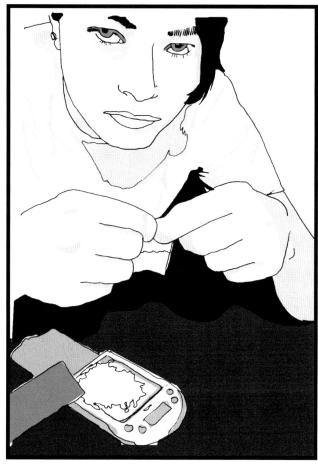

Eleanor's parents had yet to turn her childhood bedroom into the storage space/orchid nursery it was destined to become. Her bed was still there, wide, perpetually unmade, weighted down with its heavy black comforter. Glowy stars were pasted across her ceiling, posters hung from drying tape on the walls—Bjork, Bob Marley. Some flyers for poetry readings she'd been in, framed by her mother. Eleanor was a poet, a good one. She was pouring the cocaine into small Ziploc baggies and weighing them on a digital scale. The baggies were cute, they were printed with tiny red hearts. Eleanor packaged up a bunch, we dumped them into my purse and sped back to the city. I couldn't believe we'd forgot to sample some back in her bedroom. I did some inside the Jetta, a keytip full. I shoveled up another key and angled it under Eleanor's noble, Greek nose.

Back at Under A Rock the bad vibes were going strong and here we come with our own contribution. We had to wait for men to clear out of the bathroom before going in to sell the coke. That place hated women, I was sure of it, and it's partly why I didn't like to drink there. Men could do anything beneath it's claustrophobic roof, walk around naked, shoot speed up their ass, suck each other off by the urinals but you know if I got caught slipping a bag of coke to Ramona they would've thrown my ass out forever. Fuckers.

Your bags are short, Ramona said.

No, They're Not. Yeah, they are. But I Watched Eleanor Measure Them Out! They had looked a little small, but the baggies were too big, meant for clumps of pot, not powder. The bags dwarfed the cocaine. I passed the complaint to Eleanor. It's exact, she insisted. I didn't exactly trust Ramona. Once we'd bought a bag of speed together, over at a friend's house, and when we got back to Ramona's it was gone. I frantically called my friend, Did We Leave Our Speed Over There? Ramona Can't Find It. Right, my friend said dryly. She lost it. I Really Don't Think Our Bags Are Short, I said in the Under A Rock bathroom, and felt anxious knowing that Ramona was going to tell everyone we were ripping them off and then people would think we were scumbags or at least not buy from us, and then we'd never get to Greece.

I heard your bags are short, Marcia said at a party.

They're Not! I yelled. Did Ramona Tell You That? You should sell ecstasy, Marcia suggested. Everyone loves ecstasy and they're just pills so you can't short anyone. Our Bags Aren't Short, I said. They're shorter then the bindles at the Albino, she said. Well Fuck, He Sells Huge Quantities, He Just Eyes It, We Can't Do That! I whined. Plus, You Know That Shit Is So Cut. We Don't Cut Ours. We Could, I said threateningly. We Could Cut It And Make Bigger Bags If That Would Make Everyone Happy. I was very bitter, and we had only just begun our drug dealing. This was our first big party. Well, can I have a bag? Marcia asked. I'll give you the money a little later? Yeah. I slapped the plastic baggie in her sweaty palm and she walked it into the bathroom down the hall. I saw her again in a half-hour, eyes bright, nose itchy. You know I can't give you any money for, like, a few weeks? No, I Didn't Know That, I snapped. I Thought You Were Going To Give It To Me Later Tonight. Marcia shrugged. No, in a few weeks I'll get paid. No More Dealing To People Who Have Drug Problems, I fumed to Eleanor.

Later that week we were at some dingy new nightclub on Sixth Street. It was down in a basement, there were smeary colored lights and a handful of people milling about in the cavernous space. The far end of the room, back where the disco lights didn't reach, was flooded with about an inch of stagnant water. I thought that if the place was packed, if the energy was high and I was all dressed up and wasted it could be fun to dance in the giant puddle, splashing around, everyone kicking their shows off. But I was sober and tired and the puddle seemed fetid and gross, a place to breed toxic mosquitos. The more I pondered the pond-like puddle, I realized that it had possibly come from a busted sewer pipe. Were their turds floating around in the dark muck? Me and Eleanor were there for one weary reason, to sell cocaine. I wasn't terribly dressed up, and I was in need of sleep, beauty or otherwise. There was a smallish cluster of trendy-looking girls with expensive hairdos and tight jeans. They were sipping cocktails and shrieking, they were drunk. I imagined they'd squeal with glee if they knew what we were selling, but how to let them know? They were a very sealed-off clique; hugely expressive toward each other, but cutting into a sharp coldness whenever an outsider drew near. We couldn't just walk up and say Hey I have cocaine for sale if you need any. Thanks! We could bust some out ourselves and showily inhale some keybumps, but that would look sloppy or tacky or both. We were sitting in a long, dimly-lit hallway, observing the gang of girls climbing over each other on a plastic bench, waggling their asses in each other's faces. Then Paulo walked over and plopped down beside us. We only knew about this club from a flyer he'd given us at another club; this club was 'his club,' he'd said, though we hadn't seen him do anything. Some girls he hung out with were DJing, I think maybe he was 'hosting'—guaranteed to be there and say hello to you.

Paulo was one of those personalities.

Sometimes he did drag and then he was Madame Paulo. Once I saw him lip-synch to Ride the White Pony in a red leather mini-dress with buckled holes exposing skin up the length of his body. His act was a series of vogues including his pinky nail being brought under his nostril for a sniff, and pantomimed cell phone dialing time to the song's synthesized beeps. It was, like so many lip-synchs, brilliant. Thanks for com-ing! Paulo singsonged, scooting down beside us. Can I have a bag? he brought his melodious voice down lower. I'll get paid at the end of the night and get you then. Sure, I said, digging into my purse. Let Your Friends Know We Have Stuff, Too, I said, and dropped the baggie into Paulo's palm.

That means we have to stay here 'til this shit closes, Eleanor complained

. So? I said. It's Already One-thirty. It's Just Another Half-Hour. At Least We Sold Something. I walked over to the bar in the main room, scanning the dirty floor for evidence of the creeping tide. I ordered a gin and tonic. It glowed electric blue beneath the black lights. Soon the big lights were flipped on and the stark brightness swallowed up all the little colors that had been shooting around in the darkness. Time to go! the bartender barked. The DJs looked let down. I guess their club wasn't such a big smash. The bartender had become the janitor and was coming at me and Eleanor with a big broom, like he was going to sweep us up the stairs and out onto Sixth Street. We're Waiting For Paulo, I told him, and pointed to Paulo, who looked smaller and paler and generally less fabulous, blinking in the brutal light like a mole. He came at us. I'll be here all night, he said. It's going to take forever. I didn't know what 'it' was. I'd wrapped up clubs before, it wasn't a big deal. You count the money, pay people, grab your records and leave. I don't know when I'm going to get paid. He smiled a strained, apologetic smile. I'll get you later, 'kay?

We walked to Eleanor's cranberry-colored Jetta, parked on a side street in the dark alley labyrinth of SoMa. So now two people owe us money, she steamed. She said it accusingly, as if it were my fault. As if I hadn't been thinking the same thing. I Know, I said, hating how whiney my voice sounded. It's Hard, Though. They're My Friends. Paulo's' not your friend, Eleanor snapped. What? I yelped. What? He's My Enemy? You think everyone is your friend, she fumed. Everyone, the whole city is your friend. So! I yelled. So, I Have A Lot Of Friends! What, That's Bad? You don't know the difference between acquaintance and friend, Eleanor continued. That's your problem. Thanks, I Didn't Know I Had A Problem, Thanks For Clarifying That. We just started selling this shit and already people owe us money! Practically fifty dollars! That's the problem.

Paulo, she said, Is an acquaintance, not a friend.

Do you hang out with Paulo? Does Paulo call you on the phone and ask how you're doing? That's a friend. People who hand you flyers in clubs are acquaintances. What About Marcia? I demanded desperately. Because Eleanor was right, my entire roster of friends were people I had shallow interactions with at bars and clubs. Freddie was my friend but she was away, slowly starving to death in Czechoslovakia; Ramona had been my friend but now she seemed like the worst of drug acquaintances. All I could come up with was Marcia, who had me over her house every few weeks for fried chicken and videos of uncensored Jerry Springer episodes. Marcia's My Friend, I asserted. Marcia's your ex-girlfriend, Eleanor said. What, Ex-Girlfriends can't Be Friends? The Only Friends You Have Are Your Ex-Girlfriends! This silenced Eleanor, and I basked in my shallow triumph. We were sitting in the small car, engine off. Cassette tapes everywhere, crunching under my boots. I rolled down the window and lit a cigarette. All Right, I said. No More Fronting To Friends. Or Acquaintances. It's a business, Eleanor reminded me gently. I'm Not A Good Businessperson, I admitted. Well, then I'll handle it. Send everyone to me. Okay. She brought the car to life and we drove the eight blocks back to my house.

For the next three years, whenever I saw Paulo he would rush up to me and dramatically clutch my arm.

You hate me! he'd burst. Sort of a whine, sort of a shriek, sort of flirtatious. Accusing and pleading and scandalized. Paulo, I Don't Hate You, I would reply wearily. Just Give It To Me Later. The Twenty Dollars. I love you! he'd kiss my cheek and swirl off. See, Paulo loved me. That's friendship, right, love? Probably Paulo had the same problem as me; mistaking acquaintances, mistaking the entire world, for your friend. I couldn't decide if it meant I was shallow and stunted and incapable of true friendship or if I had a deeply unconditional compassion for all, the saint-like ability to see virtual strangers as a friend. Strangers are just friends you haven't met yet! I could feel the dry warmth of Paulo's quick kiss on my cheek. It felt good to have a queeny boy like Paulo single you out for a quick moment of meaningless affection. My nights were comprised of these small, ego-lifting interactions. Weren't everyone's? Paulo's persona shone especially bright , and everything he said rolled from his mouth in a lilting Latino singsong. Girl, I don't have your money! You hate me! Just forget it, Paulo, I finally said. You Don't Owe Me Or Eleanor Anything, Okay? We're All Done. Oooh! he shook his head. I love you! Maybe I had too many friends, but if you asked me, Eleanor didn't have enough.

Our drug money lived in a Marilyn Manson lunch box that was butted up against the wall by my futon. My futon was dashed in the center of my bedroom like a sinking ship. The frame had been dragged up from the street, and the flesh of the bed, the thin mat padded with a rolling sheet of foam, tufts of dust pooled in its dips and valleys, had been passed down from generations of roommates who fled the house for something better. A strip of wooden floor, painted blue, ran between the futon and the wall like a gutter, a path to the closet. The breeze of my motions to and from the dark space stirred winds that blew dustballs here and there, like tumbleweeds. Plus, there was the traffic of the mice who journeyed to my closet to nest in the thick covering of cast-off clothing that coated the floor, to feast on the old pile of halloween candy that had been spilled and then smothered by the dense pile of t-shirts and old pajamas, dresses with zippers tearing from the fabric, shit I can't believe I ever wore. That paint-stained flannel jacket, the baby-T with the red stars placed exactly over each nipple. The mice lived inside them, rutted out small, foil-wrapped pieces of chocolate, and somehow survived, though I'd heard the caffeine in chocolate was a strong enough amphetamine to kill a dog or cat.

I was scared of the hardy, caffeinated mice.

I was nervous, walking into the roomy, dark square of the closet; towels, damp and dirty, hung to dry on nails in the wall. My clothes were hung on a rack and under my feet were perhaps mice I was stomping like grapes. Baby mice, as round and hairless as grapes. I wanted to walk lightly, but didn't want to take them by surprise. I cleared my throat loudly before entering the chamber, as if sending a warning to a pair of illicit lovers that a third party had arrived. I slapped the wall with my hands.

All this traffic, human and rodent, pushed an airy tide across the floor—snarls of hair tugged out from dreadlocked tangles and clotted with tufts of glitter and stray sequins banged up against the stacks of archaic astrology books I was someday going to study. In the future, when I finally committed myself to a life of serious occult studies, after I got this writing and partying out of my system. Their cloth covers were stuck with the grime of my room and something had been spilled onto them, they'd dried in wavy warps. My end table was formerly a spool that carried wires and cables, draped with a thrifted lace tablecloth. A piece of shell sat atop it, an old beer growing mold in its dark bottle. A chunk of mirror that shone violently in the bright light of my ceiling, the jagged slash dulled a bit with a pasty coat of cocaine. On the floor, the Marilyn Manson lunch box containing the drugs and the baggies and the scale and a few hundred dollars. From the people who had actually paid for their drugs. People like Ava—friend? acquaintance?—who'd said to me as she passed me twenty dollars,

I understand, this is a business. You want money, you're trying to make money.

Yes, Ava! I had shrieked in delight, the delight of being understood by one's peers, finally. We were in the bathroom of the lesbian bar, leaning over the back of the toilet, inhaling the stuff from the porcelain, the surface gummy with old, half-peeled stickers. Our dollars were rolled tight and skinny in our fingers. Ava kept her cocaine in a tiny glass vial, the tiniest glass vial in the world. What had it been created for if not to hold cocaine, a flurry of it? I've got to get me one of those, I thought. I loved Ava, Ava was so together. Ava did everything more then me—she fell in love harder, had more sex with a larger variety of people, she drank more, smoked more and did more cocaine. And she was fine. She was a relief.

If Ava was fine then I was fine, too.

I rubbed my nose in the mirror, applied lip gloss, felt as bright as the bulb that shot out its light from the ceiling, felt brighter. The roar of the bar outside seeped through the cracks in the bathroom door, wound into me like a stream of smoke. A clamorous bar full of people and I was all of them, I was everyone, the culmination of their energy, that was me, exiting the bathroom with a smile and a numbing drip at my throat. I was beyond benevolent. I beamed at the bathroom line, the crowd of cranky lesbians, bladders bursting with beer, doing impatient, pained jigs. They were crushed up against the jukebox, they stared at me blankly, or scowled. It's not like they didn't know what we were doing in there, me and Ava. They knew what we were doing and they had their opinions about it, shifting their weight from leg to leg as their bladders swelled in unison. I made eye contact with one frowning face, rubbed the crystalized tip of my nose like giving her the finger.

I felt too good to care.

On the cover of the tin lunch box that lived on the floor, Marilyn Manson is all powdered up like a geisha, with shattered-glass contact lenses in his eyes and a black slash of mouth, black slash of hair. I opened its buckle and pulled about four hundred dollars from the wad of money bound up with a ponytail holder. Our Greece money. The more we focused on Greece the further it felt from this soggy town and its yeasty bar culture that bloated us with alcohol, lured us to its jukeboxes nightly to invest dollars in the very same songs, each night a rerun of the last, the only changes perhaps being which person hits the crying point by last call.

We kept our love in the Marilyn Manson lunch box like a wild bird, rare and tropical, one that had to be smuggled to its native island and released to the air, sent to fly among the olive trees, sent to explode in the hot glare of white wall and blue sky, blue sea. Greece, a whole land of blue. We would stay with Eleanor's family who of course would not care that we were gay. They would accept me readily, because I was with Eleanor, I was family. My Greek family. I'd always wanted to be Greek.

I thought perhaps I looked a touch Greek.

No, Eleanor said bluntly. She had her You're Fucking Kidding Me face on. Maybe Italian? I tried. I pulled my long blue hair back from my face. Look At My Eyes, I insisted. My Eyebrows. Don't You Think I Look Like I Could Be Mediterranean? You're tripping, Eleanor said. I released my hair, let it bounce back into my face.

We took the Greece money, most of it, and invested in ecstasy. We bought a polka-dotted plastic bag filled with chalky white pills.

Drug packaging is really adorable.

I thought the ecstasy was a better drug to be selling, karma-wise. More in line with the buddhist notion of Right Livelihood. Cocaine was bad, it was a drug that convinced you to buy more of it, a virus that turned your will against itself, that colonized your best intentions. After the initial rather mild euphoria petered out all that remained was compulsive storytelling and the urge to snort more.

Since we'd begun selling the stuff and consequently inhaling more of it I'd taken to telling and retelling the same Marilyn Manson story.

It had been weeks, perhaps a month solid that I had been repeating this story. I told it nightly, in the room above the lesbian bar where the cocaine-addled friends of the bar gathered after last-call. Sitting around the storage space, filling it up with cigarettes and chatter while downstairs the bartender counted her drawer. Whoever was the closest friend of the counting bartender would descend the stairs to fetch extravagant rounds of free drinks, to quench throats so dry they caught on themselves. I would launch into my story, the one Marilyn Manson show at the Cow Palace where he rose from the floor on a flickering cross of television sets that burst into flames; how I was on ecstasy and had peaked at the exact moment Marilyn came to the edge of the stage on a pair of four-legged stilts, how he reared up straight like a mythical beast, raised his huge, stilted arms into the strobe-lit stage lights and howled I'm never gonna save the world for you, the lights cutting through him, holding him in an egg of blinding glow, his fake eyeballs flashing in his face and I almost stopped breathing. I'd talk about how when he did that third reich bit that disturbed everyone he was really trying to demonstrate something about the insidiousness of fascism but it went over the crowd's head, the crowd being primarily fourteen year old Hot Topic shoppers trying not to puke up all the beer they drank in the parking lot before the show.

I would turn to Marcia and Ramona, who had been at the concert with me and were always upstairs at the lesbian bar after last call, and I'd ask them—Really, Didn't You Feel Like You Were Witnessing Rock And Roll History? It was great, they'd agree, my old friend Ramona who had told the world my bags were short and my old friend Marcia who still owed me twenty dollars. Every night I would ask them to confirm the brilliance of that one Marilyn Manson show I was so passionate about and every night they would say yes. Okay, we know, you love Marilyn Manson! someone laughed, and suddenly I was mortified. I really talked about this every night. I was boring everyone, had deeply bored them weeks ago, was now a joke. Cocaine was so intense, I had to stop doing so much of it.

No one would ever understand how great that concert was. I just had to accept it.

Selling ecstasy would be great because I wouldn't want to do a lot of it. It's too big of a commitment, being that high. It was such a spooky drug, how it filled you with lush sensation one minute and then the next you were skirting the void, tipping on the edge of the big scary, the ultimate nothingness that Buddhists talk about but trust me, it doesn't feel so peaceful when it's yawning like a cosmic tar pit in your psyche. Ramona, an intense Sagittarius who was apparently comfortable jogging back and forth between deep pleasure and stark terror, tried selling ecstasy once and it was a total joke. She'd drink too much at the bar and suddenly it was ecstasy time. The tiny pills would get pulled from her pockets and enter her mouth. Worse, they'd enter my mouth. Open up, she'd slur. I Don't Have Any Money, I'd object. Ecstasy is so expensive, and you can't measure it out over time like a bag of coke. With ecstasy ulp it's gone. Don't worry, don't worry, pay me later. I'd drank too much, too, and my mouth would hang open, ulp. Guess I'm not sleeping tonight. A few weeks later and the big dealer would show up, down from Vancouver to collect his money and Ramona wouldn't have it. She'd call around; suddenly I owed her forty dollars. Shit, I Have To Pay For That? I hadn't understood. I'd scrounge up half of it. The dealer would be so completely pissed. Ramona had eaten half the stash herself.

We weren't drug dealers, me and my friends. We were drug users.

Me and Eleanor got rid of most the ecstasy in one swoop at one of Ava's giant parties.

We sold what we brought and then ate some ourselves. Someone snapped a Polaroid, me and Eleanor melting into a beanbag in Ava's bedroom. All doped up, our eyes half-lidded. It was minutes before we waddled out to hail a cab. I'm wearing a long, gauzy robe, sheer pink, over a slip. It was a wedding-themed party and my costume was that of a bride in her honeymoon suite. Eleanor wore a suit, her hair shot up thick above her baby-smooth forehead.

We ate some more a week or so later, shut inside my bedroom. I had cleaned it up a little for the occasion, bought giant tulips, grape popsicles and mint Nat Shermans to smoke. The thing about ecstasy is it really makes me want to smoke but also leaves me sensitive to the ultimate disgustingness of cigarettes, so I had to smoke really nice, clean ones. It was like sipping on little puffs of soft, minty air, the Nat Shermans. It was divine. My bedroom was gorgeous, a red light bulb glowed from a lamp, casting tulip shadows onto my wall. Ooooh, I pointed at the silhouette, whispering, as if my voice could startle it, drive it away. The languid bend of the stalks. Oooh. I loved being on my bedroom. It was so safe. The only thing I had to do that night was sleep, eventually, and I was already there, on my futon. Beautiful. My room held me in its crimson glow and I was deeply, cosmically in love with Eleanor, we would sell these pills and find our way to Greece, where we would be better, freer, more beautiful. I barely felt the looming void that night, only hints of it when I left the warmth of my room and moved down the gloomy hallway to the bathroom, or to fetch a grape popsicle from the kitchen. I decided

I would always keep grape popsicles in my freezer.

They were only the best thing in the world. I wished I had more of them. I began to have scarcity issues about the popsicles, there in the frosty gust of the freezer. There were only two left and I was far too high to walk down the street to the twenty-four hour Foods Co. for a new box. The void flared open beneath me. I ran down the hallway and pushed my bedroom door open with a squawk. It didn't matter. We had those great cigarettes. The tulips drooped romantically in their jar of water.

Clearly we were not good drug dealers.

When we sold through the rest of the E we were done. Still, the phone rang. It was Christopher. Hey, I heard you were selling things, that hesitant voice, like maybe the phone was being tapped. As if. The phone was cordless, heavy and black. Sometimes we got crossed wires, but all the talk was in Spanish. Could I come over . . . ? Christopher trailed off. I have some friends with me. I didn't even know Christopher had my phone number. This is how things take off, I remember thinking. I was sitting on the couch in the living room, watching tv. Our cable was about to be shut off, we hadn't paid the bill in quite a while, maybe had never paid it. No one presently living there knew how we had gotten cable in the first place. The bill came addressed to an old roommate's old girlfriend who was now a man living in southern California. I cursed me and Eleanor's impatience. We only had to get our thing down, or sales schtick, our personal business philosophy of no fronting to friends, no mistaking acquaintances for friends, no more apologizing for the size of our bags and no more doing the drugs we sold. No more being too lazy to get out there and push our product, to be a recognizable presence in bars and nightclubs. We only needed the patience to wait out that early period and then our phone would begin to beep, people would come to us. That's how it worked.

Real drug dealers sat in plush chairs in private apartments,

they had a ring of people who admitted and dismissed buyers from their chambers. They were not lingering in pathetic discos in rotting neighborhoods smiling desperate and creepy smiles at potential users. We could've stuck it out, conjured up some dignity. The phone was jangling, our number was out there. Someone else called, I'm a friend of Ramona's, she passed me your number, can I come over? But the Marilyn Manson lunch box was dry. It contained only the props, the bags and the money. No, I'm Not Doing That Anymore, I spoke regretfully into the receiver. Oh, the girl regretfully responded. We hung up.

The intense planet Pluto continued it's tangoing transit on my person. How, how could I make some money? It seemed it would have to be something dark and illegal. I had no other options. It wasn't my fault, it was society. Don't forget that. I wished I could make a prostitute's salary and have a prostitute's daily structure without actually being a prostitute. What if I turned tricks part-time, one or two a week, stashing the cash in the Grecian Getaway lunch box fund. I would keep my job at the bookstore, it wouldn't become my life, not like before. It wouldn't be so surreal and stressful. It would be occasional—strange, but not my daily fabric.

I was having so much sex with Eleanor, we couldn't stop.

I had scratches on my cheek from when she fucked me against my glittered bedroom wall and the sharp topography of sparkle cut into me and I didn't even feel it.

I was feeling too much, I was feeling everything. Eleanor had bruises on her cheek from where I bit her. Our limbs, our arms and legs, were mottled with teeth marks, we looked like spoiling bananas. We looked like we beat each other, and we did. It would become too intense and my fists would rain down onto her chest, or she would grab the skin around my ribs and pull like she would tear me open if she could. I'd have let her.

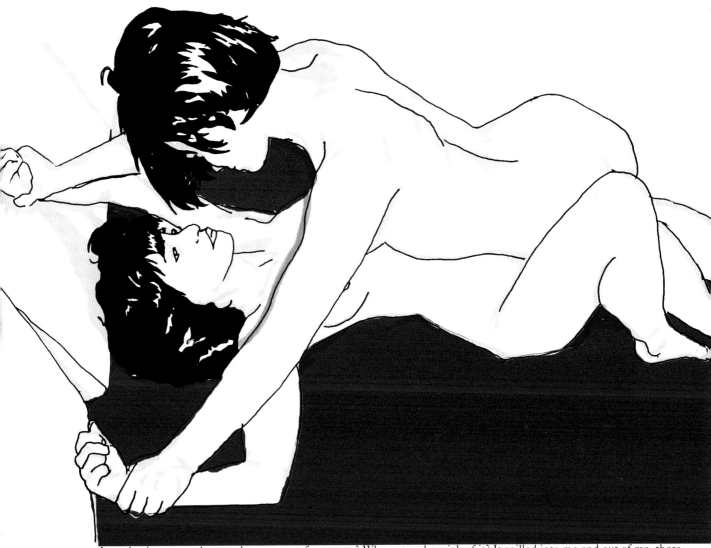

I was having so much sex, why not some for money? Why not make a job of it? It spilled into me and out of me, there was so much: sex like water, self-generating, self-perpetuating, obsessive-compulsive Pluto transit sex. But I didn't want to share any of it, especially not with strange, gross men. It would be beyond wrong. If only we could bottle it, the pheromone fumes that rose from our bodies. We could do shows, I thought. Surely men would pay to see this. Real lesbian fucking, the deep and brutal reality of it, hands plunged into unbreakable cunts, none of those gently skimming tongues, no rosy tumbles, this hard and scary sex, **this exhausting, painful gorgeous sex.**

At a poetry reading sponsored by the local paper's personal ad supplement we picked up an application. We were giggling, we held the Xeroxed form and a nubby pencil and together we brainstormed. Eleanor was all but a boy, and we couldn't have that. Eleanor would have to be a girl, there was no way around it. She was eighteen, which she'd have to have been even if she wasn't. How Old Do I Look? I asked. I relaxed my face, turned it toward her. I removed my glasses. You look seventeen, she said. No Way, I Mean It, Tell Me. You look young. It's Not True. I Have Wrinkles. I was twenty-nine years old. Too young to be an older woman with a Mrs. Robinson draw, too old to be the vaunted age of eighteen. Can I Be Twenty-Four? I asked. Definitely. Twenty-Five, I said. Twenty-Six. I wrote the word twenty-six on the form. Twenty-six was still young, right?

Wild Young Lesbians, our headline rang. Want To Put On A Hot Show For Generous Gentleman,

it continued in regular type beneath. I would be Daisy. I imagined myself in a shirt tied into a halter beneath a rack I did not have. I imagined an ass that rolled out from a pair of cut-offs. It was a stupid image, but I went with it. Eleanor was Gina. She was busty, she was fresh out of high school. We walked back to the table, handed in what was, essentially, our job application.

We drove out to Daly City, to get a beeper. We had to drive through Colma to get there, the famous city of mostly dead people, acres of cemeteries spanning out from the freeway. In Daly City the beeper store curved on a corner, and inside a lady sold us their cheapest plan. We selected a used beeper, probably traded in by an upgrading teenage girl. It was translucent periwinkle, stuck with glittering stickers of flowers and cats. I liked us having a beeper. Mostly Eleanor carried it. Beep me, she'd say, and I would. I'd call the number and punch in 1-4-3, which was popular teenage code for I Love You. It appeared that I would never actually grow up. I was giddy, punching in the numbers from the phone at work, at the information desk at the rear of the bookstore. My bookstore was in the Castro and most of the people who shopped there were gay and male.

We sold a lot of porn.

The new Harry Potter, with a side of porn. The Hours and porn. Mrs. Dalloway, plus porn. Body for Life and porn. That's what we sold. David Sedaris and porn. Wallpaper magazine and porn. A man lingered, impatient, at the info desk counter, straining beneath the weight of his French Laundry Cookbook, brought to me for gift-wrapping. I was on the telephone, ignoring him. I hit the buttons—1-4-3—I slammed down the phone. I felt about fifteen years old, perhaps I always would. When I finished wrapping the giant cookbook, topping it off with a great, curling ribbon, I'd stand in the metaphysical aisle pretending to organize while looking up all I could about Eleanor's sign (Libra), her Chinese astrological sign (Goat), and how it vibed with me, an Aquarius Pig. One book promised that together we could create our own little world. The outside world would drop away, comparatively bland, its colors blanched by the bright blast of our combined romantic imaginations. I drifted over to the travel section and grabbed some guide books to Greece, took them back to the info desk to study.

The personal ad supplement had given us a phone number to access our voice mail. On Wednesday the papers came out, and there we were—Wild Young Lesbians. The men called in a steady trickle, leaving hesitant messages. We would return their calls, leave our beeper number. Beep Us, I'd speak into their machines. Sometimes they'd answer their phones. I did the calling. Eleanor's voice was too deep, she sounded like a man and plus she was shy and had never interacted with men this way, never had conducted this particular exchange. I would phone them and say Hello, This Is Daisy, I'm Returning Your Call? Why did I want to speak in a southern accent? It was so embarrassing. I resisted the urge. I trained my voice to sound like the voice of the happiest girl in the world, the sweetest, the best girl, the girliest, least threatening lesbian ever. I confirmed what the ad had promised—I was young and wild and my girlfriend was even younger, possibly wilder. We would come right into your home and have sex atop your bed. It was like live porn, there in your very own bedroom. They couldn't touch us but they were welcome to touch themselves. I made it sound like I was granting them a rare privilege: you will actually be allowed to touch your very own penis! Something they no doubt did multiple times a day was now wrapped in an air of decadent luxury. Pay us two-hundred and fifty dollars to not make you come. You will do all the work and we will ignore you. Most guys weren't biting. We're A Specialty Item, I said to Eleanor, full of optimism. We're Not For The Average Guy Who Just Wants A Fuck. We're Something Else. Eleanor looked discouraged. The beeper was like sixty dollars, lifted from our Greece money. One guy called and asked Will you jump up and down on my chest in a pair of sneakers? Oh We Would Love To! I squeaked. And my back, you'd stomp on my back, jump up and down and crush me? Uh-Huh! I chirped. Uh, he groaned. Ew! I shrieked, and hung up the phone. I was calling on the cordless.

I had to remember to block caller ID each time I returned a call.

Other men didn't understand the phrase 'generous gentleman.'

They thought we were just some lesbians who liked to have sex around men, thought they were the perfect guy to observe such a spectacle, thought they were living in a fantasy world where things like this actually happened. No, Sweetie, I said. You Pay Us. Money? a guy asked. And I can't . . . touch you? That's Right, I purred. I'll . . . think about it. The phone clicked. Shit. Finally we got one. His name was Norman and he lived over in the East Bay, in Oakland. He gave us his address, it was by the big lake over there, we had an appointment for Friday at six PM, and he didn't flinch at the two-fifty price tag.

NORMAN
510 - 714 - 4150

Friday night, four, four-thirty and Eleanor's in a slip. I've got bunches of them, different colors. I wear them outside, they're cheaper then dresses and look great, though once an old woman at the thrift store glared at me and told me to go home and put the rest of my clothes on. This particular slip that Eleanor is wearing is lavender, and there are scraps of pale lace sewn to the nylon, at the tits and at the hem. I let out the straps to accommodate Eleanor's bosom. It is large. It is strange how large they look in the slip, the thin material straining against and lifting them. Usually Eleanor wears industrial-strength jog bras that smooshed them down into a nondescript secret breast pile, and then she piled some t-shirts on top of that, and then the top t-shirt, and then a sweatshirt. Now they were like two fruity orbs, they swayed there on her body, ripe enough to drop. I set some heeled shoes onto her feet and began dealing with her hair. It was short and thick and generally sprung up from her head in clumpy spikes, but that would not do, not with the lavender slip. The slip I would never again be able to wear, not after seeing how good it looked on my girlfriend. The fabric would be just the slightest bit looser, puffing around my own scrawny tits, haunted by Eleanor's rack. I grabbed a small, greasy container of pomade and pulled a mound of the petroleum hair gunk loose with my fingers, rubbed my hands together to soften it, and slapped it down on Eleanor's hair, a series of cowlicks. I tamed her hair, it grew oily and perfumed, it lied across her forehead and I clamped it there with a metal clippie. I pulled some wisps out toward her dignified, masculine face, to soften it.

Makeup was tricky.

Absolutely she needed it, but too much and she'd look like a drag queen. I dusted her with some pink and made her terribly long eyelashes thicker and darker.

I gave her a purse and a coat, my torn-up rabbit jacket I bought off a homeless guy for seven dollars while drunk, back at the start of my Pluto transit. I should have done her nails, but there was no time. Oh My God, I said. She turned to the chipped full-length mirror standing in my corner. It Is So Perfect That You Are Gina, I said, But Dolores Would Have Been Even Better. She looked like a cross between the Italian girls from East Boston who always wanted to kick my ass for looking at them when I was a teenager, and a hooker straight out of Donna Summer's Bad Girls. It was the tiny fur coat. It couldn't be buttoned over her heaving chest.

All right, I said. I wrote down Norman's probably fake name, and his East Bay address, and stuck it on the fridge with a magnet. If We Never Come Back, Make Sure They Arrest This Man! I hollered out into the house. The girls staying in the back room, the middle-class college girls who liked to say they'd been 'cut off' from their parents for being queer, emerged from their closet. I liked them all right, but it was always hard to hear people complain about being 'cut off' from some sort of money supply. Especially when they were still driving around in a big-ass jeep, had credit cards, and shamefully smuggled a cell phone in their back pack, all funded by the irate parents. They were staying with us until they found jobs and housing, but mostly they seemed to smoke a lot of pot and sit in the living room making beaded jewelry. The more dominant half of the couple, Brooke, had once grabbed my ecstasy stash and put it in the freezer without telling me. I'd had a stressed-out panic attack, running around my cluttered, cruddy bedroom, hurling dusty CDs and knocking over half-empty bottles of beer looking for it. Oh I put it in the freezer, Brooke said, with the casual air of the stoned. It's better for ecstasy to be in the freezer. Our freezer was currently crammed with all manner of items which thrived in freezers—film, cigarettes, vodka, pot brownies. I worried about Brooke weaving hemp necklaces on our sofa for the rest of my life. She seemed to have job standards. She wasn't just grabbing a job and trying to make money, she was holding out for a good job with nice people that paid well and utilized the training she'd gotten at her university and provided her with benefits and the opportunity to rise up through the company. I thought she should just buck up and buss tables like the rest of us, but here I was, off to fuck my girlfriend in a strange man's bed. Brooke handed me her cell phone. The words Brooke's Secret ran in digital type across the little screen. Take it with you just in case, and call if anything happens, we'll answer the phone.

God, that was nice. Thanks, Brooke, I said. I slipped her small phone into my army bag with the rubber whip, the dildo and the harness.

We got lost in Oakland.

Again and again we circled the big lake, passing joggers, the sun going down in the pale sky. We pulled into a convenience store for directions. I hated climbing out of the car in my skimpy black slip, my giant leopard shoes. I clop clop clopped inside, the little bell announcing my entrance. Dudes at the counter turned to me and looked, I glared and snorted, marched across the stained linoleum to the beer cooler at the back. I grabbed a single bottle of cider and clomped back up the the counter, slammed it down surly like a cowboy. I hoped. The cashier eyed me warily. Do You Know Where Dransom Street Is? I asked, pulling a couple dollars from my canvas bag. Careful not to tug out a stray condom or a black lash of the whip. Dransom Street? the man repeated, staring. Yes, I'm Looking For Dransom Street. The loitering man to my left observed me quietly. I hate when people look at you like you're a whore and you actually are one. It makes me want to kick their teeth in. In my ginormous patent leather platform shoes bought for cheap at Hot Topic I was actually taller than both guys, a towering Amazonian whore. Forget It, I said, and stormed with my cider out of the market.

They Don't Know Anything, I snapped, hurling myself back into Eleanor's car. Of course it was not her fault that we were lost, but I wanted Eleanor to triumph in all the areas I was deficient. I couldn't drive, Eleanor drove, therefore she must know how to drive everywhere. She was a Bay Area native, therefore she must know where Dransom Street was. I looked at the clock on the dash. We're Fucked, I said. The cider was a twist-off, I yanked the serrated cap free and tossed it with the debris at my feet, sipped the calming tangy bubbles. Are you made at me? Eleanor asked, tense. Her lips were a smear of lightly sparkled pink gloss. I felt a roiling, directionless rage. At the men for looking at me, and then, uselessly, at Eleanor. For not having offered to go into the market herself. Why should she? She was wearing the same get up as me, and was doing the driving. Plus, I had more practice wearing such outfits, could walk in my heels. I was not in a costume. I dressed like this all the time. I thought, I deserve a prize. A gigantic prize I'm never going to get, for being a female in this world. For being the kind of female I am, for getting so much shit all the time, for surviving. I deserve a prize. One better then a bottle of cider. It's glass was cold and wetly reassuring in my tattooed hand. I'm Not Mad At You, I said. I'm Just Mad. I Feel Weird, We're On A Call. I felt suddenly intense. I didn't know how to be about it. My attitude toward sex work toppled between cavalier lightness and super extra heavy duty whoa. Now that the silly, sparkly dress-up portion of the night was concluded, now that we were lost in Oakland, lingering outside a crappy liquor store, being stared at through the grated window buy the curious eyes of some bored, alcoholic men, now that we were late to sell some aspect of our sexuality to a random dude,

I thought it was time to get intense.

I drank my cider. Eleanor stared
at the bottle like it was a hitchhiker I'd brought
into the car without asking. Hey, she said, If this isn't going to
be fun, let's not do it. Fuck it. We don't have to. Jesus, why wasI
acting like such a damaged hooker? Was I being oppressed? I was going to
fuck my girlfriend and get paid. I drained the last of my cider. Let's Drive Back
Over By The Lake, I said, my voice wobbling with forced optimism. It's Got To Be
Right Around Here. I Feel Like We're Right On Top Of It.
Norman lived in an apartment on a block filled with shrubby, boxy apartments, identical. no wonder
we couldn't find it. We parked around the corner and clambered out of the Jetta, straightening our
outfits. We looked really trashy, and the neighborhood looked clean and calm, sort of suburban
despite its location in America's murder capital. I lifted my empty bottle from the car floor and
placed it gently in the gutter. Slowly, together, we clip-clopped down the street, climbed a small set
of stairs, entered the apartment building. I looked at the address penned onto a scrap of torn paper.
Number eighteen. I hit the bell. Eleanor clutched my hand, we folded our fingers together, the skin
of our nervous palms sticking moistly. Hello, a scratchy voice burst staticy from the metal speaker on
the wall. It's Daisy And Gina, I hollered. Sorry We're Late! The buzzer honked and we pulled the
door open, trod the orange carpet down to apartment eighteen.

Behold Norman.

He is white, he is balding. I'm bad with ages but I'll guess forty-nine. A lot of our callers had gone into elaborate descriptions of their appearance, detailing their weight and physique, their race and their hairstyle, assuring us they were both clean and attractive. I found it both boring and irritating, these unnecessary monologues. We weren't paying them for sex, what the fuck did we care what they looked like? And they were lies besides. None of them were attractive, I'd bet money on it. The most I'd hope for was clean. Norman hadn't gone on any such spiel, which I thought was very professional, and he looked clean, though not attractive. he wore a Polo shirt and khakis and wire-rimmed eyeglasses framed his small, mousy eyes.

Hello, hello, come in, he greeted us. Hi, I'm Daisy. My hand shot out and wrapped around his soft, surprised palm. This Is Gina. Hi, Eleanor murmured. Please, come in, take off your coats. Eleanor slip the bunny from her shoulders, revealing her excellent tits.

That was two-fifty right there.

I tugged off my own coat and tossed it to the floor.

We were in what appeared to be the living room, but a giant futon was opened up in its center, our stage. I got the place nice and warm for you, he said quickly, and bent to shove a rolled-up towel against the front door, to keep the outside air from sneaking in and cooling off the fiery hell that was Norman's apartment. The place was warm. A fire flashed in the fireplace, hot wind blew out from the baseboard heaters, and there were little glass candles everywhere, flickering. That Was Very Thoughtful, I stammered. Thank You. The little glass candles were apparently scented, the air was a hot collision of musk and cinnamon, fake berry and tea rose, like the inside of a burning Hallmark store. I was glad we'd both worn slips. Can I get you some water, Norman asked. Yeah. And Can We Take Care Of Business? Of course, of course.

I followed him into the kitchen, divided from the main room by a little breakfast nook. He dumped water from a Brita into some glasses, then pulled his wallet from his khakis and counted out two-hundred and fifty dollars. Yes. Thank You, I smiled. I took it all back into the main room where Eleanor sat on the edge of the futon, her high-heeled clogs kicked off. I slid the bills into my army bag and turned to Norman. So, We Should Just Get Started? I asked brightly. Eleanor looked slightly bewildered. We hadn't really mapped out how it would work. Um, please, yes, Norman said. God his house was hot. And the radio was tuned to The Quiet Storm, the smooth songs for lovers station, groovy soul tunes. I nodded for Eleanor to move back on the futon and I crawled behind her. I pulled my slip from my body and peeled Eleanor out of her lavender casing, freeing her tits. I figured I'd leave my shoes on, just for the glamour of it. I removed first my thong, then Eleanor's thong which was of course really my thong as Eleanor didn't wear thongs, she wore men's underwear like a normal butch girl.

It was mesmerizing to see Eleanor in this get-up.

It was like being in a dream, it was a different Eleanor from a parallel universe, a female, girl Eleanor with a body that sprung golden tits and sparkling lips. I sunk my hand into her cunt. She gave me the mean face she made when we fucked, it thrilled me always because it resembled the cruel boys of my youth who had wormed their way into all my fantasies, and now she looked like their bad-ass sisters and girlfriends and she was on her back with my hand lodged between her legs, pulling and tugging on her nipples like stretchy toys.

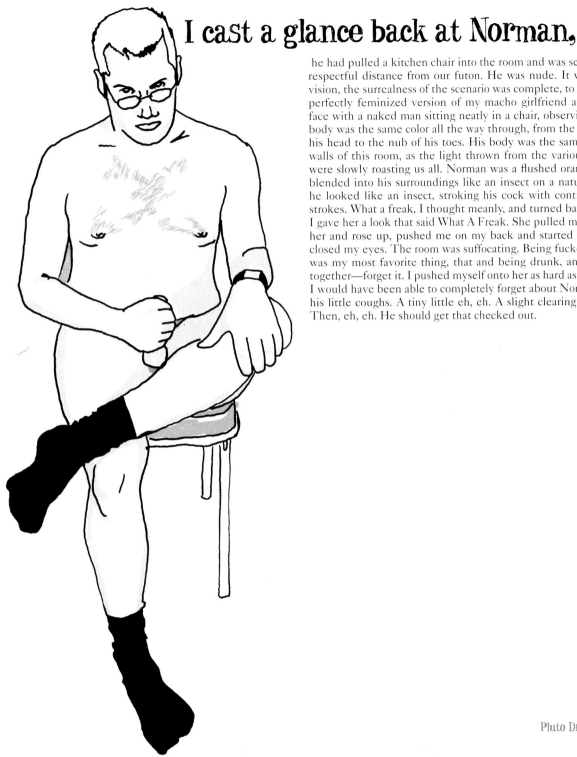

I cast a glance back at Norman,

he had pulled a kitchen chair into the room and was seated at a very respectful distance from our futon. He was nude. It was an absurd vision, the surrealness of the scenario was complete, to turn from this perfectly feminized version of my macho girlfriend and be face to face with a naked man sitting neatly in a chair, observing. Norman's body was the same color all the way through, from the bare crown of his head to the nub of his toes. His body was the same color as the walls of this room, as the light thrown from the various flames that were slowly roasting us all. Norman was a flushed orangey color, he blended into his surroundings like an insect on a nature show. And he looked like an insect, stroking his cock with controlled, careful strokes. What a freak, I thought meanly, and turned back to Eleanor. I gave her a look that said What A Freak. She pulled my fingers from her and rose up, pushed me on my back and started fucking me. I closed my eyes. The room was suffocating. Being fucked by Eleanor was my most favorite thing, that and being drunk, and both things together—forget it. I pushed myself onto her as hard as I could stand. I would have been able to completely forget about Norman if not for his little coughs. A tiny little eh, eh. A slight clearing of the throat. Then, eh, eh. He should get that checked out.

Me and Eleanor kept switching positions—it was a show, after all.

We went down on each other, so he could witness this ultimate lesbian sex act, and also so he could get a good look at our asses. I even spread my cheeks for him, bonus. I felt an odd affection for odd Norman. he seemed afraid to get too close, which I liked, and even the excessive heating on our behalf was endearing. Though I'd always thought there was something emotionally and ethically wrong with the men who pay women to let them fuck them, I thought it was actually fairly healthy and moral to pay for a show like the one me and Eleanor were performing. We weren't having to compromise our bodies, we were doing something we loved to do, and we were barely having to fake anything. I mean, Eleanor's femininity was a sham, and I couldn't focus enough to have a real orgasm, but next to the complete facade of prostitution this was totally sincere. I'd pay a couple girls who were totally in love with each other to fuck in my bedroom, I thought.

Norman had a very polite, very subdued orgasm into the palm of his hand. He pattered into the kitchen, washed, and returned to his chair. About a half an hour had gone by, we had thirty minutes of high-powered fucking left to go. Norman lit a Marlboro and rested it in smokeless ashtray. The ashtray whirred a little smoke-sucking whir and Norman coughed his delicate smokers cough, eh, eh, and Eleanor slipped a finger into my ass, which was aimed in Norman's direction. I yelped.

She pulled my hair and stared me down.

Our normal sex life was fairly violent, involving slaps to the face and the hurling of wicked insults, but we were afraid to indulge in such passions lest we scare the mild-mannered customer. Position shift—kneeled on the futon, so much firmer and cleaner then my futon at home, which seemed like a smooshed cotton ball next to this luxurious model. I fiddled with my boobs while Eleanor laid beneath me. Without my glasses it was hard to make out the expression on Norman's orange face, but I think he was bored. One hand hovered over the cigarette, the other cupped his shrunken penis, sort of shyly, I imagined, or perhaps he wanted to spare us the sight of it. I wondered if he wanted us to wrap it up but didn't want to hurt our feelings. I faked a big orgasm and fell back onto the bed. Eh, eh, Norman coughed. He wasn't completely naked, he had his glasses on. Thank you, he said softly, our cue to quit it.

I felt exhausted. Normally after such an extreme workout we'd both pass out, and truly I wanted to drift off on Norman's quality futon and take a nap. Eleanor wiggled out from under me. Can I use your bathroom? she asked. Down the hall. I collected my things, yanked my thong back up my thigh, arranged the strip of cloth neatly in my ass crack. Excuse me, he said, and walked into the kitchen carrying a folded bundle of clothes. Eleanor returned. She'd dressed in the bathroom, was all covered up. I snatched my slip from the carpet and walked the hallway to the bathroom. A small room yawned darkly to the right of it, I peeked in. A single scented candle lit it full of shadows,the shadows of a bunch of excersize machines. It was a little gym. Crazy. The candle bobbed atop a nautilus machine, and beyond that, the source of Norman's consistent, orange coloring—a tanning bed, its lid stretched open. It looked like a dim little cave full of dinosaurs , these hulking machines. I stepped into the bathroom, also lit by a single scented votive. I sniffed the air. Vanilla. Norman was totally nuts about candles. I pulled on my slip and didn't concern myself with my hair, fucked into a rat's nest at the back of my head, or my smeary makeup. It was time to go. Call Us Again, I said to Norman as we stepped out into his hallway. It felt like Antarctica out there, after all that time in the furnace of his apartment.

Well? I asked, back in the Jetta. Eleanor was cruising up a ramp that aimed us toward the Bay Bridge; San Francisco sat across it, misted in fog like some mythical city, like Avalon. I was anxious to get home to put on pajamas and watch cable. Are You Okay? Yeah, totally, Eleanor grinned. He gave you all the money? I pulled out two-fifty, slapped it in my palm. Yup. He was so weird, Eleanor said. The way he jerked off and then washed up. He Was So Prim, I agreed. He Didn't Want To Get Himself Dirty. I Bet He's A Germaphobe, I said. I Bet He Can't Actually Have Sex With Women Because It's Too Messy. He Just Likes To Watch From A Distance. And he's a compulsive excersizer, Eleanor chimed in. Did you see that shit in his room? The tanning bed? The excersize machines? It's like a small gym! And The Candles! I shrieked. We Didn't Talk About The Candles! The car was filled with our cackling. I Think During The First half Hour All He Could Think About Was That There Were Lesbians Fucking In His Bed, i said.

And During The Second Half Hour All He Could Think About Was That He'd Given Us Two Hundred And Fifty Dollars.

We thought that for future calls we would offer our customers different scenarios. Do You Have Any Fantasies You'd Like Us To Act Out For You? I asked.

We Can be Schoolgirls, We Can Perform An S/M Scene For You, We Can Be Nurses...

I tried to think of costumes we could whip together fast and cheap, and also worked at imagining the characters that populated these men's fantasies.

Me and Eleanor's own games—older sister's boyfriend/younger sister, or older man at hotel pool/young girl—would never work.

Mostly the guys seemed embarrassed, unprepared to share a hint of fantasy. They also seemed unprepared to schedule an actual call. There were lots of curious callers, scared callers, broke callers or slightly crazy callers.

One guy sounded like he could come through. H is name was Jonathan. I'm pretty attractive, he promised. Great, I pushed the word through my clenched jaw. Here's Jonathan's story, since he told me all about it: Jonathan has a fiancé and he really loves her. he doesn't want to cheat on her, but Jonathan likes action and adventure and variety. Our service would be perfect, he said, because it wasn't really cheating. It's Not, I agreed. It was totally sneaky and would probably creep his fiancé out and make her feel heartbreakingly inadequate, not to mention unable to trust another man for the rest of her life, but was it cheating? No, not technically. I honestly didn't care about the specifications of their heterosexual commitment, I cared about me and Eleanor going to Greece. It's not cheating because I don't get to touch you, Jonathan continued his rationalizing. Right? I don't get to touch you? Absolutely, I said with great firmness. No Touching. But You Can have us Do Whatever You Like.

Jonathan said to meet him at a hotel out in this neighborhood that has a lot of hotels, a big curving boulevard that swerves out toward the water. In my bedroom our heels snap and bang against the wooden floor. I fixed Eleanor's hair again, snapping down her tough locks with a barrette, smoking up her eyes, rouging her lips and we're off. The hotel we arrived at was under construction, which meant we had to parade past a small crew of carpenters, all who turned to gape at us. Our plaid skirts swished beneath our asses, the frills of ruffled lace on our ankle socks were ridiculous, clearly we were hookers. The stares didn't bother me, though. Maybe because it was daylight and we were in public, it's own safety; maybe because I'd have stared at us too. Or maybe I had swung back the other way, into the giddy, getting-away-with-something feeling of sex work, of doing something fantastically illicit, if not illegal.

I grabbed Eleanor's hand and together we climbed the stairs that took us to 4B.

Knock, knock, here's Jonathan.

Jonathan's a yuppie. His hair is longish, curling. He's lanky, a bit nerdy—half yuppie, half computer geek. He's a dot-commer. He's got glasses on, he's young, like thirty-five. He's wearing jeans, he's happy to see us. Oh, hi! he exclaimed like we were old friends from college. We crammed into his little hotel room. The carpenters sounded like they were right outside his window, the building shook with the slam of their hammers. How does this work? he asked eagerly. Well, We Should Take Care Of Business First, I said crisply, and he handed over the money. Oh, I have wine, would you like some? I had refrained from a pre-call cocktail because it would have felt too alcoholic, drinking during the day, but now it would be part of the call. Yes, Please, I gushed, and accepted a plastic cup of white wine. Jonathan took a sip. Pretty good stuff, he said cheerily. Yeah, It Is, I said with mock thoughtfulness. Who cared? It could've come from a box for all I knew, I didn't drink for the taste. You two look great, he said. Really sexy. Thanks. There was an awkward pause. Were he supposed to say that he looked sexy, too? He didn't. He didn't look sexy. Why Don't We Start? I suggested. So, I just can't touch, right? Right. You Can Touch Yourself, Not Us.

On the bed me and
Eleanor made out
furiously, occasionally
pulling back and being all
tonguey and lesbian for
dude.

We unbuttoned each other's blouses, pulled tits from the cups of bras, lifted skirts to squeeze handfuls of ass.

When our clothes were tufted on the questionable hotel carpet I leaned off the bed and pulled the strappy leather harness from my army bag, the beige dildo with its understated veinage bobbing in its slot. I climbed into it and pulled the worn black straps, the metal loops pressing tight against my hips. Remember when Madonna said in Interview about how ridiculous she felt when she strapped on a cock and tried to have sex, angering millions of lesbians? I sort of understand what she was saying. For certain I do not think it is ridiculous when a girl straps one on and comes at me with it. That's serious. Especially if they're growly, especially if they look like they want to eat me alive. But me in a dildo, me, myself, it is harder to take seriously. I do go forth and bravely fuck despite this lack of confidence, I ignore the sensation of silliness and swallow the question clotting in my throat like a bad bit of food: Can you really take me seriously in this? I do not ask. I just get to it and fuck and generally, after a few minutes of it, the question melts, the worry evaporates and I am not so much silly or self-aware as I am sweat and hair and mouth and teeth and muscle. I turned to Eleanor and pushed her legs apart.

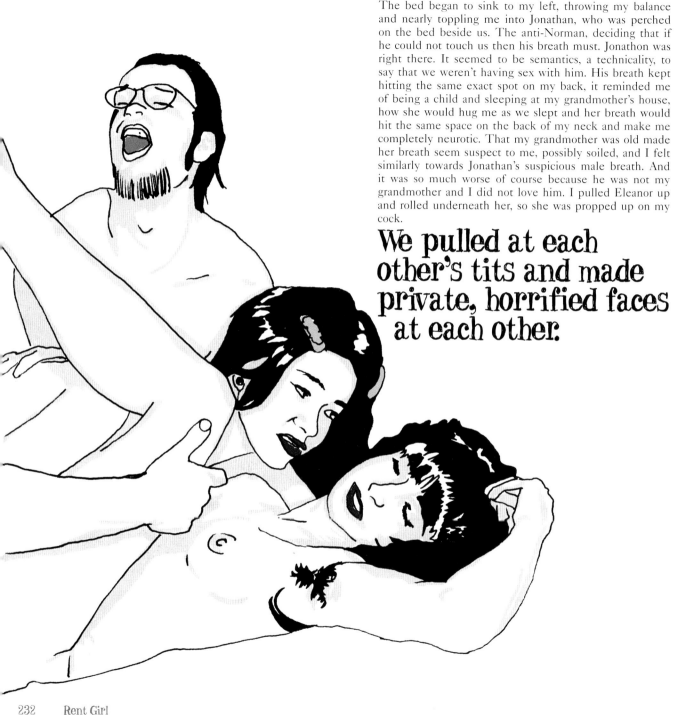

The bed began to sink to my left, throwing my balance and nearly toppling me into Jonathan, who was perched on the bed beside us. The anti-Norman, deciding that if he could not touch us then his breath must. Jonathon was right there. It seemed to be semantics, a technicality, to say that we weren't having sex with him. His breath kept hitting the same exact spot on my back, it reminded me of being a child and sleeping at my grandmother's house, how she would hug me as we slept and her breath would hit the same space on the back of my neck and make me completely neurotic. That my grandmother was old made her breath seem suspect to me, possibly soiled, and I felt similarly towards Jonathan's suspicious male breath. And it was so much worse of course because he was not my grandmother and I did not love him. I pulled Eleanor up and rolled underneath her, so she was propped up on my cock.

We pulled at each other's tits and made private, horrified faces at each other.

Every position we flipped into, there was Jonathan,

his big, inquisitive head rising like a cartoonish balloon in the corner of my eye. He had a big, engaged smile on his face, like a kid at the zoo. When his head rose, his breath followed, coming in steamy pants syncopated to the beat of his beating off. The bed shook with the movement of his elbow. What if his stuff got on me when he came? Oh my god. I kept my eye on his wank, and continued to maneuver me and Eleanor away from his fumey breath and eventual ejaculation. Why had we thought we could engage in sex work and somehow avoid grossness. Norman was a fluke. There we were with a regular, red-blooded heterosexual male with no germophobia or issues with feminine odors, and he was going to get every fucking penny's worth by leaning way in and hoping we might accidentally bump into him. Norman would only happen again if the original Norman called again, and the chance of Norman ever beeping us again was fucking slim, as we had left him in a state of vague regret at having gotten so little for his money. Puff, puff, from the spot on my body Jonathan's breath was hitting I calculated that his face to be southwest of my pussy. I imagined a giant Plexiglas sneezeguard, the sort that canopy salad bars, sheltering me and Eleanor's bodies, conjured a psychic, white-light protective barrier between us and his shuddering, unpredictable maleness.

It ended without Jonathan bumping us or spraying us with his muck. An expert lurker and loomer, he managed to stay on the edge of too close for the entire call, and contained the inevitable result of his jackoff—not as delicately as the uptight Norman, but he took care of it. Later I stood in the room, buttoning my shirt up over my chest and its tiny, pretend bra. Eleanor was shut into the bathroom, sink streaming noisily. Outside the carpenters drew near. Their constant pounding, along with the sugary crash of the sweet pale wine had given me a headache. But the wine, along with the exertion of fucking and being fucked and effort of avoiding Jonathan had made me dizzy and drunk, emptied out, fuzzy inside.

That was cool, Jonathan said dumbly. He was smiling his perpetual smile. Thanks, Glad You Liked It. You're really attractive, he went on. It was so cool to see someone so feminine making such masculine gestures. it was wild. . . . Yeah, I said. Do you two ever flash? In Public? Flash? I asked, thinking maybe I wasn't hip to yuppie sex lingo. Like, show yourself to strangers, in public. Wow, he meant the old-fashioned flashing, like geezery dudes holding open their trench coats and waggling their peckers at children and young, strolling women. Yeah, Sometimes, I lied. Do you ever go to the Marin Headlands? Um . . . I Was There A Couple Times, I said. I recalled a green path, looking for deer below on the hill or seals bobbing in the bay. That would be a great place to flash. Yeah, You're Right, I nodded. I mean, it was true. A flasher's paradise if you cared about such things, which I did not. Maybe you'll be there this Saturday? His eyes behind his glasses held mine behind mine.

No, I Don't Think So. I smiled a cheap smile.

The bathroom door opened and out came Eleanor. Her regular, surly vibe had returned. The call was over and she didn't really need to say goodbye, she just raised her chin to him sharply, a challenge.

God, Could He Have Gotten Closer! I shrieked in the car.
Did you look at him? Eleanor asked. No! I Can't Really See
Them Without My Glasses Anyway, But I Don't Want To
See Their Cocks And I Don't Want To Make Eye Contact.

I look at them, Eleanor said.

I look them right in the eye, I catch their eye while they're looking at you and look at them like, yeah, you keep looking motherfucker. Keep looking cause you are never going to touch it. That shit's mine. She tugged me in for a hot kiss. Our lips were all smudged up.

It was the day our ad ran out in the paper and we hadn't renewed it. I knew we wouldn't. we were lazy and forgetful and I knew in my heart that the psychic end of this road was as bleak as the dead end of the more involved sex work I'd done before. The novelty would wear off and what we were doing would be laid bare as work, and work made the funnest activities rotten, we hated work, Eleanor and I. Never did I want to be worn out and tired, frustrated and broke and showing up to fuck my girl like punching a time clock. This would be our last call.

We had to visit someone who would appreciate the spectacle of Eleanor in a plaid skirt and a clippie in her hair, a faceful of cosmetics.

We went home, to Brooke and her paramour weaving bracelets in the living room. We're Done, I announced, and let them pour us vodka tonics and gasp appropriately at our hilarious getup and daring occupation, let them toast us and cheer our love before we left to spend a chunk of our earnings on steak dinners and goblets of wine. We counted the whole of our money, the drug money and the sex money, and there was maybe enough to pay for one ticket to Greece. But there was more then enough for us both to go to Disneyland, so we went there instead.

Thanks

Michelle wants to thank the incredible Annie Oakley for her tireless work on behalf of raggedy queer sex workers everywhere, and for her friendship. Same goes for Scarlot Harlot. Thanks to my immensely supportive sister Kathleen Tomasik, and my very inspiring friends--Peter Pizzi, Sara Seinberg, Tara Jepsen, Jessica Lanyadoo, Ali Liebegott, David West, and Clint Catalyst, to name a few. The deepest and most colorful thanks to Laurenn McCubbin, for her vision. I mean that metaphorically and literally. Thanks to Bucky Sinister for being so Bucky about it. Thanks to Sash Sunday. Deep and abiding thankfulness to Eileen Myles.

Laurenn would like to thank Jen Loy, Antonia Blue and Jeff Johnson for being SO patient and kind, Warren Ellis, Peter Rose, Matt Fraction and Kelly Sue DeConnick for being the best support group ever!, the SK8 Jesuits for distraction and arguements (Dan, Chu, Jeremy, I am looking at you!) Lauren Martin for being her pretty, pretty self, Adam Hatch and Tim Brown for the inspiration and conversation, Bucky Sinister, Ron Turner and everybody at Last Gasp for all the help, Prozack Turner for the fly threads, and to Michael McCafferty she would like to say THANK YOU, from the bottom of her heart.
Thank you to Michelle Tea, for giving me something so amazing to work with.
Special, super HUGE thanks to Tristan Crane, without whom there would be no book. Thanks for keeping me shooting, mister.

Special Thanks
Laurenn and Michelle would like to thank our models, especially Megan Fenske, Jezebel Kuono'ono Lee, Mona Coots and Tristan Crane. Thanks to everyone who contributed to this book!

Carl Reidlinger
Amanda Strain
Brent Goodbar
Nick Botto
Robin Abad
David Sterry
Jamaica Dyer
Marc Nordstrom
Justin Hall
Ted Naifeh
Jen Loy
Sherilyn Connelly
Katrina James
Alex K

Andrew Gill
Allegra Lundy
M Trucco
Aaron Farmer
Andi Stou
Cat
Adina Morguela
Jenna Feldman
Scott San DiFillipo
Mike McCafferty
Arshad
Tara Goe
Katherine Keating
Pat Spurgeon